PRIVACY
LOST

—— PART 1 ——

PRIVACY
LOST

—— PART 1 ——

EDWARD M. PLUT

BookBoro
A Neighborhood of Writers and Readers

Published by BookBoro Press
Pittsburgh, Pennsylvania
www.bookboro.com

Distributed by River Grove Books
Cover images used under license from
©istockstock.com/Margarita Khamidulina

For ordering information or special discounts for bulk purchases, please contact Greenleaf Book Group at PO Box 91869, Austin, TX 78709, 512.891.6100.

Publisher's Cataloging-in-Publication data is available.

Print ISBN: 978-1-7376140-0-5

eBook ISBN: 978-1-7376140-1-2

Printed in the United States of America

First Edition

To my sons and forever wife: *Privacy Lost* was conceived when our family became complete; you inspire me to do my best. Putting words down to describe how I feel about all of you, and how you make me feel about myself, is impossible. Love, pride, respect, gratitude, worthiness, peace, happiness . . . there are simply too many words. Rather than obsessing over the words, I hope to continuously show you how I feel.

Note to reader: If you're a careful reader, or a hardcore sci-fi fan, skip this prologue for a better experience. If you want a more casual experience, read on and read carefully.

PROLOGUE

In the year 2045, implantable technology that allowed human beings to live to our full biological potential was perfected and regulated. It was expensive and only available to the wealthy—the very wealthy. After a period of global unrest, at the start of the Great Transition, implantable technology was made available to the masses through advertising. Wet advertising, commonly called wet ads, are advertisements initiated from within one's body.

The innovation of ad-based implantable health technology allowed anyone who desired a longer, healthier life to receive an implant. Wet ads are regulated by the federal government and strictly limited to sensing and simulating a person's senses and emotions in order to influence purchasing decisions. Over time, this technology advanced, allowing humans to live much longer. Some humans, the wealthy, live much, much longer.

Through the Great Transition, there were two hundred years of sustained global crises and wars as economies, industries, and infrastructures adjusted on an unprecedented scale to the impact of extended human longevity. The world adjusted to a self-induced inflection point in the evolution of our species. Along the way, the implications of advanced artificial intelligence threatened the human condition. Errant self-aware AI created crisis after crisis, threatening our lives.

The Human Lives Conservation Act elevated the army to act as an independent body; its only purpose is to protect human lives from all other threats. AiiA, the Artificial Intelligence Investigation Agency, is the branch of the army on the front line, responsible for stamping out errant AI threats.

Now, in the year 2420, Implantable Health Assistants are the most advanced technology created by our species to date.

Has anything really changed?

THURSDAY, MARCH 26, 2420
07:00:00

As Miles begins to wake, he takes a deep breath and feels humid, salty ocean air fill his lungs. The sensation of sandy wind on his skin and perception of gentle beach sounds quickly evaporate from his awareness. He opens his eyes and turns away from the light coming through the window of his small apartment in Columbus.

He opens his phone, looking down at the projected screen that appears bright and tangible at the intersection of his extended index finger and thumb of his left hand. Miles makes an audible sigh of acknowledgment, feeling sad—no, he feels disappointed—by the reality of the wet advertisement. Even with his specific education, Miles's mind cannot always differentiate his own innate senses from the wet ads, push notifications, and reminders initiated from within his body.

He looks at the banner ad on the top of his phone:

NORWEGIAN'S PANOCEA CRUISE LINER
100 Times Bigger and more Luxurious than the *Titanic!*
Reserve your spot for its maiden voyage in 2421.
The earlier you book, the more you save.
Book right now and save 40%!

What's the *Titanic?*

Miles triages the wet ad, as required for premium wet ads like this one, setting a reminder for the next time he speaks to Shelby.

He looks at a text from his friend, Ray: "C me ASAP."

Miles sits up on the edge of his bed, looking at the dense cityscape of massive glass and stone buildings through the window. The city looks like a frozen moment of evolution; buildings seem to grow taller and more extravagant in the same way plants grow to compete for sunlight and rain. Like the way blooming flowers attract pollinating insects, the architecture seems to be meant to attract occupants. Miles stands and uses a bottle from the table next to his bed to spray a uniform row of green sprouts emerging from the soil in the base of the window.

Why does he grow these plants? They serve no purpose.

He turns and steps through the open doorway to his left and into a sterile, functional-looking living room. A simple couch, chair, and table appear permanently fixed to his left, while a conspicuously blank wall is directly in front of him.

A motion from his right hand sends the call request from his phone to the image wall facing him. A green light next to Ray's name indicates his friend is currently open to receive a call from Miles, and the connection is quickly rendered. In stark contrast to the blank wall a moment ago, the room now explodes forward into bright color and motion as Miles's view now extends into a much larger outdoor patio. His friend Ray, a clearly fit man at the peak of his youth, is running on the patio's marble surface, although not moving toward the lawn in front of him. Sunlight shines directly from above the garden and the walls are covered with thick green leaves and a myriad of colorful flowers.

They have talked four times since January and both friends admit that they should speak more often. Miles always feels eager; Ray's view is not usually rendered, and Miles feels joy when he comments about the scenery during their calls.

Ray slows his pace to speak. "Miles, thanks for calling. You're gonna get a kick out of this! Oh—" he stops speaking abruptly, as if forgetting something important that he intended to say. He then continues quickly. "Have you seen that *anthropanic philanthropist* again?" he questions, or jokes perhaps? Ray's next footstep moves his body a step toward Miles as he steps off what is now clearly a moving panel below him.

"How long have you been waiting to use that joke?" Miles responds.

"Only since you first told me about her," Ray says, smiling. He was joking.

"Shelby. She's a professor of Anthropogenic Evolution—you know that. I haven't seen her again yet. We had a great time though." Miles exaggerates, as he felt hopeful but mostly uncertain that night. "We are planning to get together again next week for dinner," he lies; they have not set any specific date to see each other again.

The first time he met Shelby, on a date—an odd expression—she explained Anthropogenic Evolution to Miles as if talking to a child. Miles does not read poetry to compare and understand, but it's probably similar to Shelby's description that day. She is a data scientist who studies the impact that extended life is having on human civilization. Even though she studies the impact on the tangible world, she, too, is working with virtual information and data to understand the world around her. Fascinating.

"She sounds great from everything I've heard. You know I'm just kidding. Make sure you keep her attention; she's the only interesting thing about you right now, Milton!" Ray jokes.

"Jerk," Miles says, feeling embarrassment when hearing his real name. He has often told others that his father provided him little more in life than a funny name; he corrects others when they call him Milton. The two friends have also joked about Miles being verbose and generally bland, a compounding of undesirable traits. Their joking seems mutually appreciated and respectful, in ways, as they say, only close friends of fifty years or more can understand.

"You still seeing the lawyer?" Miles asks. "I hope not; she's way too smart and attractive; your kids will resent you for diluting their gene pool." He jokes.

"Ha ha! Yes, Jules, yes I am . . . we are . . . whatever," Ray says uncomfortably.

"You're *whatever*, huh? You're sixty-one now, my friend. It's time, as they say, to start thinking about settling down, having a family," Miles says.

"Actually, I'm really torn. I love her, I do, but she's thinking about a second family," Ray says, looking sincere. "I even heard her talking to her daughter about how great it would be to get pregnant together. I'm not even thinking about a first family. And, honestly, when I do," he continues, "I think I want to go through it with someone as ignorant as I am."

"That's pretty ignorant, my friend. Good luck finding that match," Miles jokes again and continues, "Well, you know, Jules is like eighty or eighty-five, right? They all want another round of kids at that age these days."

Ray smiles. "How's your mom, by the way? Wasn't it her 120th last week? Is she still on an ad implant?"

Implant—not exactly the precise word, but that is the common terminology.

"One hundred thirty last week, actually. She's doing well," Miles says. "I pushed her to withdraw from our group retirement plan to go ad-free, but she actually likes the wet ads. She doesn't want to invest right now, maybe never," he shrugs.

"In fact," Miles continues, even though Ray seems about to speak, "she was so happy the other day when she smelled lilac from a wet ad. It brought up memories of her mom, her childhood home. I guess she used to spend hours talking with her mom under a lilac tree in her backyard as a kid. She now has a subscription to some lilac shampoo."

Ray looks down at his phone momentarily.

"Anyway . . ." Miles seems to take notice of Ray's attention and speaks more quickly, feeling compelled to finish. "She likes the little reminders, even if it's only to buy corn flakes. I just don't know how she stands the relentless McNuggets *smells*."

Miles flexes two fingers on each hand as he says the word smells and continues, regardless of his friend's inattentiveness. "She's directly between two fast-food terminals; it's hard to visit. If you move to the other side of the room, you have repeat wet ads from the next terminal."

Miles still continues, but with a different tone, "She asked about you the other day, you know. She would love to see you. Vic and Little Ray are *sixteen and fourteen* now," he emphasizes and pauses. "If you can believe it's been that long." He finishes and seems to be trying to make eye contact with Ray.

"I know, I need to. I will," Ray says with a sincere expression, but also reluctance, perhaps, before he looks away.

"Just call . . . or go," Miles says after a short silence. "*You* will feel better, and . . . she loves you like her own son. You saved us that day. You couldn't have saved—"

"Stop," Ray replies quickly, looking at Miles not with anger precisely, but something else—perhaps determination. Miles has started this conversation one other time. "But I will; I will talk to her soon, I promise," Ray says, seeming to return to purpose.

"Anyway, the reason I really wanted you to call," he nods at Miles, projecting impatience. "You'll want to hear *this*!" Ray says, and Miles feels excited. "Secure Channel. Listen to this."

The Secure Channel option now encrypts and only stores data on each of their phones until the end of the call. Ray leans toward Miles as if he believes they are in the same room; the rendering is convincing.

"You know the new upload entertainment stuff? Where they upload your consciousness, then run a simulation and let you watch how you would do in a movie or some other situation that your avatar thinks is real?" Ray asks.

"Yeah, you upload a copy of your mind to see if you can survive the Hunger Games?" Miles responds with a question of his own, even though he clearly knows the answer.

"Hunger Games?" Ray asks with a look of confusion.

"Oh, some old movies my grandmother loved. Basically, a bunch of kids are dropped in a jungle to hunt each other. It's just the first thing I thought of when I started hearing about those simulation-movie things where you upload *yourself.*" Miles is flexing his fingers again.

"Well, anyway, I got pulled into a new unit that's just forming," Ray says.

They have spoken frequently about their time together in the army; Miles has said many times that he just followed Ray. Ray had a specific purpose, but Miles had no better ideas at the time. Miles discharged after ten years and has said that he only went to medical school as a reasonable decision. Miles is an ER doctor, little more than a maintenance tech, fixing minor injuries and maintaining Implantable Health Assistants, or IHAs, or *implants*, as they say. Miles feels regret almost daily. With the IHAs, there is no real practice of medicine any longer, at least not outside research. Ray, on the other hand, an understandable expression, has been in the army thirty-five years. He just qualified for AiiA four years ago, a rare and admired profession people speak about often. AiiA is the Artificial Intelligence Investigation Agency administered by the army; people say "I Yuh" when referring to it. Ray's stories are always very interesting.

"So, there are supposed to be controls in place," Ray continues, "so that your avatar or whatever doesn't wake up and realize it's in a simulation, right?"

"Well, of course," Miles says, and Ray smiles.

"Turns out, the controls aren't a hundred percent," Ray says. "Some of the uploads are going crazy and disrupting the sim. But that's not the big problem." He is speaking more quickly as he continues. "Listen to this! Some uploads are becoming self-aware, waking up in the simulation, begging and demanding not to be deleted!" he says. Fascinating.

"Wow." Miles feels surprised.

"I know! In this one sim, the one based on that superhero movie—the one with the actor with the hair in his face all the time?"

"Oh yeah, I know that movie..." Miles responds, staring ahead at Ray, but his vision is not focused as Ray continues to speak.

"Shoot, I can't remember his name," Ray continues. "Anyway, this simulation is based on that movie where a group of campers get hit by a meteor and they all wake up with superpowers they have to figure out. In the simulation, you get to watch how you, or *your copy*, would figure out his powers and then how he would live life in the simulated real world, with these newfound powers. You have to give the production company some video data so they can create a deep-fake. They use deep-fake technology to stitch together what you and your normal world would look like for the simulation. So that *the you* in the simulation thinks it's all real and that he has these powers that nobody knows about.

Then the *real* people get to watch the simulation like a movie and they see what *they* would have done with those powers. Beware, by the way. People are finding out some pretty dark shit about themselves when they watch the replay, some of the things they find out they would do with—"

"PowerPlay!!" Miles interrupts abruptly. "Holy shit, it's funny, I just had a wet ad for that simulation the other day and thought of that same guy. I wondered if my upload would have that hair or if that me would think to get a freakin' haircut."

"Yes, that's exactly the one I'm talking about!" Ray confirms. "So, this group of friends who did the sim together all woke up, six of them. One of the uploads was a coder who somehow figured out how to send a stream of the simulation to *himself*, while it was still running and before the company could delete and rerun it. The company has been deleting and rerunning sims for who knows how long. By the way, if you ever do one of these and get a refund with a message that you can't watch your simulation for some reason, that means your avatar probably woke up. Seriously." Ray has an expression of disbelief.

"Huh," Miles says.

"*They* ..." Ray now makes a similar gesture with two fingers on both hands as he continues. "*They* are insisting they have rights as self-aware, conscious, sentient beings, or whatever. Some are demanding to communicate with *themselves* or a lawyer. Congress is pulling together a whole new division in the Department of Infrastructure. They don't even know what to call it yet." Ray pauses for a moment. "And of course, we are forming a new division at the office." Ray uses this word in reference to AiiA's headquarters, the Pentagon. Miles often jokes about Ray's use of this reference; Ray now says it more frequently as a result. "*They* are always a threat, even if we don't know what *they* are yet. Things are just getting organized, but it's going to be wild. I'll keep you posted."

"Wow, that's crazy," Miles says.

Self-aware copies of human consciousness in a programmed simulation. Interesting.

"Well, I think we were right to treat AI as a formal threat early on, no question. And this is probably no different," Miles responds, but he's not feeling conviction. He's more intent on influencing Ray into elaborating. He likes these conversations.

"I know we're doing the right things. Don't get me wrong, we could never keep AI under control with business sanctions. I just always wonder about what could have been, had we not gone so far," Ray says.

"It could have been Skynet, terminators," Miles interrupts, still likely trying to excite his friend into saying more.

"I guess. But maybe not. Do you remember that prequel they made way later, the one that showed how Skynet started?"

"Sort of, they showed how it learned and took over."

"Yeah, I just don't know that we had to go so far with the limits on AI development. In that movie, they actually predicted, all those years ago, a pretty accurate timeline and threshold for self-awareness. I watched it again the other day and I just can't help wondering why they can't figure out how to control or throttle their progression. Instead of the limits we have. Or, I guess we did, since things like this keep happening," Ray says, oddly changing his own mind. "I wonder what someone like Shelby thinks," he says while looking more thoughtful, but Miles interrupts this time for a different purpose.

It's not jealousy, precisely, that Miles is feeling. His feelings are complicated and difficult to interpret, but Miles does not feel good about Shelby and Ray meeting.

Miles interrupts, "You know it's funny; I was just thinking about asking her if she wanted to try the murder mystery simulation. That looked like fun. Although I think her upload would figure it out in no time; mine would end up being the victim somehow. Maybe I'll ask her on a cruise instead."

Miles feels relieved to be interrupted as he receives a message tagged "Work" and "Immediate." He opens the message:

Emergency Room surge in 28 minutes; Individual transport pods en route to the ER are currently 42% greater than average; Vitals and biomarker sensors on mass transit routes all within normal limits. Report immediately.

Miles orders himself an individual transport pod to arrive in twelve minutes with a confirmation of the pick-up time suggested.

"Sorry, Ray," Miles says. "I wish I could ask you some more questions—not that you'd tell me much more anyway, none of the *really* good stuff anyway. But I gotta go."

Then, speaking quietly and seemingly to himself, "What the hell? Doesn't look like another quick-flu." Quick-flu is a common virus, not typically life threatening, but that evolves too rapidly for any model IHA's antigen technology to be effective.

"Is this another surge of weird accidents? Hope it's not another Hell Day. But it's just the individual pods coming in this time . . . ," Miles says even more quietly, no longer paying attention to his friend.

"Well, talk to you later, Miles. Sounds like you'll have your hands full. Hang in there," his friend says, filling the silence three seconds after Miles abruptly stops talking. Ray does this frequently when they talk.

"See you, man," Miles responds dismissively as he ends the call, walking toward the bathroom at the same time. The sudden end to the rendering of the green patio is disorienting. It also gives Miles a momentary sense that the room is . . . imploding, that might be the right word.

THURSDAY, MARCH 26, 2420
07:32:38

Miles opens his phone from within the interior of the transport pod. He renders his phone's screen and an additional data feed to the front window. Most days, he chooses a global news stream rather than watching the world around him pass by at confusing speeds. Miles is not looking directly at the screen ahead of him where a female voice is questioning the CFO of LifeTrust Corporation; LTC +4.25% per the scrolling text at the bottom of the screen.

The voice is asking about the impact of the company's latest nanotechnology on first-quarter revenue. Instead, Miles's attention is focused on the red status light next to a rendering of Shelby's face on the left margin of the screen. The smiling and frozen face in the periphery of Miles's vision shows a young woman, her bright, almond-shaped and intelligent eyes capture attention easily, even out of focus. Even so, Miles focuses on the red light for an unusual period of time.

His focus is broken when the pod slows noticeably as it nears a terminal. Although he just ate breakfast, Miles receives the familiar hunger sensation that immediately precedes a wet ad for food. It feels more like a vague shadow than a true sensation of hunger to him; however, the smell that follows is unmistakable and specific: fresh, warm cinnamon buns, or more specifically, the complex mix of chemical reactions and neural transmissions that are unmistakable to Miles's brain as the brand Cinnabon. He even senses the warmth of the bun as though it really existed. Miles enjoys the sensation with the start of a smile while he dismisses the wet ad and directs the pod to continue to the ER with a single motion on his phone.

He looks back to Shelby's image and smiles fully as she is now shown as available on his phone; the indicator light he has been focusing on is now green. He calls her, and puts the call up on the windshield screen.

Miles's heart races as Shelby's piercing eyes look up from her desk. She greets him with what they call a warm smile, another odd expression.

"Good morning, Miles," Shelby says as she slides the screen on her desk away, seemingly intended to show Miles that he has her full attention. "It's early for you, right? Everything OK?" she asks.

"Good morning, yeah, yeah, it's fine, just have to go in early, maybe another weird round of accidents again. I don't know, since the mass transit stats are normal—" Miles stops himself from elaborating. "You're in early too. Ooh, does that mean you found your next project?" he asks, feeling genuine interest.

"Ugh, I wish," she responds. Ugh? "I've been helping a few colleagues with some data mining until I feel inspired. Just procrastinating, if I'm being honest. I still can't decide; I want something big that I can immerse myself in for a few years, but then, as you know, I'm thinking about a sabbatical," she says, with more meaning in her eyes that they both seem to understand. They connected last month through a company's application that matches busy professionals who are looking to start a family with a like-minded and loving partner.

As Shelby explained on their first date, she is a freelance researcher who participates in one of the largest science and technology collectives in the world. Shelby understated her position in the collective at the time, but Miles learned in the pod ride home that she has been a highly renowned and followed data scientist in both academic and business professions for fifty-three years. Shelby explained that being a part of the collective allows her to focus on research she cares about, not all the business and financial implications of her work. She said it's complicated, but scientists, coders, engineers, and anyone—in her words—can contribute their research, inventions, and data to the collective, even building off one another's work to drive constant innovation. Corporations and governments can draw from this collective at any time to drive the development of new technology or any commercial use. Everything in the collective remains open source until a commercial use case is identified. At that time, shared ledgers are created for the intellectual property, or IP, and all contributors receive fractional ownership and royalties based upon the value of their contributions. All the license terms and algorithms for determining value are pre-negotiated by the collective.

It's not that complicated, although she apologized even before explaining the research collective to Miles on their first date. When she poured herself and Miles the final glass of wine that night, Shelby commented that she had done very well with some data mining projects that led to new targeted-marketing techniques. She gets a share of incremental profits from any ad campaigns that leverage her work. With some embarrassment, she admitted she only does this kind of work because she is saving to invest in an ad-free IHA.

She also admitted that her status with the research collective was the only reason she had a regular paying gig, a strange word she used at the time. She is paid by the university where she is a tenured professor. The hospital where Miles works is part of the same university organization, and they spoke at great length about how they have similar feelings of disappointment about the work they do. According to Shelby, the university is little more than a certification body these days.

Her work with the university is more of a job she practically has to do, which is understandable. However, her focus has been on trying to identify and start her next research project with the collective. She described her research as the work she needs to do. She is compelled to understand the world around her, which is more of a secondary purpose, but also understandable. Shelby told Miles that she is looking for something big and meaningful for her next project. She then immediately contradicted herself by saying that she should be doing something more commercial. Curious.

"I'm well aware of the potential sabbatical," Miles responds with a smile. "But you don't have *any* ideas?"

"*Any* ideas?!? Unfortunately, *that's* not the problem. How much time do you have?" she asks, but also, somehow, she isn't really asking.

"Um, twenty-two minutes seven seconds, at least for now," he responds after glancing at the time to destination, Cleveland.

"Careful what you ask for, twenty-two minutes is a long time," she says quickly back.

"Try me! I have the attention span; I can go for twenty-two minutes," he says, pausing only momentarily before continuing. "Tell me a few things you're thinking about; who knows, maybe I'll have something deep to say," he says, smiling.

"Alright, I'll try to bounce two or three ideas off you and see what kind of insightful things you have to say." Raising an eyebrow, she continues, "So, my leading idea for a new project is this: I'd like to study and understand why we, as human beings, have allowed companies so deeply into our lives, into our bodies. The influence companies have on us—that influence is inseparable from our own humanity."

"Definitely deep," Miles says, and Shelby laughs.

"See, I told you, careful what you ask for!" she says, now with a new type of smile. "I want to understand and explain why we have allowed corporations so deeply into our lives, into our bodies. That wasn't a conscious decision we were given an opportunity to make. It was more of a passive acceptance, after a billion tiny influences on us over a long period of time. I want to figure out and explain all the important contributing factors about why we are willing to give away so much of our autonomy . . . so easily." She pauses, as if expecting a question. It seems as though she has explained this more than once.

"What do you mean, *a billion tiny influences*?" Miles asks.

"I mean, centuries ago, we started allowing corporations to monitor our communications. We allowed them to start passively listening to and analyzing our private conversations and messages, to follow our location, track everywhere we went. We essentially allowed companies to follow, scrutinize, and analyze *ALL* of our activities and decisions. And people accepted this, willingly, easily. And do you know what *we* got in exchange for giving these companies all our valuable data?" she asks, again pausing for a moment. "More relevant advertisements." Another pause. "That's it; people got ads that were more relevant to their hobbies or whatever they liked instead of random ads."

"More relevant ads? That's all they got?"

"That's right. We don't own our data today, because we started giving it away from the very beginning and every day since. We gave it away freely to the companies who were marketing to us, so that they could sell more effectively to us. What does it say about us to make that kind of exchange? Willingly? How did we start there . . . and now we allow these companies inside our bodies, driving us toward decisions they want us to make, steering us in the directions they want us to go?" She sounds more excited, and again as though she has spoken about this many times.

"Hmm," Miles signals he is listening; he is now feeling uncertain.

"Today, we allow marketers inside our bodies to influence us. Yes, we now get something a lot more valuable than more relevant ads, because we can live longer, healthier lives with the implants. But our lives are now sponsored by companies whose explicit purpose is to profit from us. But we didn't get to make this decision in any conscious way. We started passively accepting this decision four centuries ago with small and seemingly insignificant decisions. We clicked away a part of our humanity with every checkbox agreeing to terms and conditions that we never read. Over and over, we agreed to new terms and conditions that were slightly more insidious than the last time we checked that box. I want to understand all the key factors that would contribute to acceptance of something like this on a worldwide, massive scale. Who will we be as a species in another four or five hundred years? Will we have any free will left?"

As he listens, Miles is alerted and looks down briefly to activate his phone. He snoozes the bright and conspicuously flashing Norwegian cruise reminder from this morning. He immediately clenches his right fist in frustration, but doesn't make a sound. Shelby doesn't continue after noticing Miles's frustration and distraction.

"Mr. Twenty-two minutes, huh?" she asks, while appearing to communicate dissatisfaction to Miles.

"Sh...shoot. I just snoozed a wet ad I had this morning; I meant to dismiss it. Now I'm going to have it again. I'm sorry; I'm listening, I promise," he responds.

"Ah, perfect! You're making my point for me! I want to identify all the key contributors to why we, as a species, have accepted extreme consumerism like this into our lives and bodies."

"*I*, as in me, made a point about extreme consumerism?" He is confused, but projecting a smile.

"Have you ever noticed that we all say *I HAD an ad?* In the same way we say *I had an idea?* You said it just now. That's sad when you think about it, right?" She waits for Miles to respond.

He pauses, feeling genuine surprise. "I guess I never thought—or noticed."

"The fact is, there were a number of certain tiny influences over a very long period of time that have led us to accepting *this.*"

"*This* being precisely what?" Miles asks.

"*This*—meaning the acceptance that an advertisement is now fundamentally part of our humanity. That we can no longer differentiate an ad from a thought or an idea of our own. I want to understand more about how we came to accept this. We actually accepted this centuries ago— before implants, by the way. We need to identify and uncover influences that might be working on us today, before these influences take hold of us in an irreversible way." Her expression is difficult . . . vindication maybe.

Miles interrupts. "I don't think I'm smart enough to earn a second date."

Shelby is immediately amused again and Miles proceeds. "Dumb question, but you can understand something like that from data?"

"Absolutely. You just have to be clever about how you slice and dice it in order to understand what secrets the data hold."

"You have to dissect it to understand it? Like a cadaver?" he asks.

"Ha, clever. In a way, yes. You have to be able to dissect the data and get to the heart of the underlying problem you're trying to solve. And we have unthinkable amounts of data about people, about the world around us—data to understand cause-and-effect relationships. We have data going back hundreds of years; we can study almost anything about ourselves and the world around us. It's probably easier to think of things we *can't* do with data than to begin to explain how much data we actually have and all the things we *can* do with it."

"I think I want to take your word for that," Miles jokes.

Shelby bites her lip, as if trying to hold back a larger smile. "So, my second project is very similar—"

"What!?!? We're only on the first?" Miles jokes again, and they both laugh for a moment. "I'm sorry; go ahead," he finishes.

"OK, well, so the second option is just a different flavor of the first, but in this case—"

"Can we call this Project B?" Miles asks. Shelby looks impatient through a near smile, a smirk, as they say. "Sorry, go ahead for real."

"Fine, Project B. It's just like the first, but instead of looking at our acceptance of extreme consumerism, which is sort of passive acceptance, I would be looking at more of a conscious decision. I want to understand the most important factors in play for building a consensus on an extreme idea by such a large population. The obvious thing to study is our mass consensus on AI, the army, AiiA, and all that."

Miles now feels the kind of intense interest he feels when having a conversation with Ray. He tilts his head quickly and asks, "What's the obvious part about that?"

"I mean, as a species, we came together before it was too late, in most people's opinions anyway. We came together as a population to radically limit and control artificial intelligence. The Human Lives Conservation Act elevated the army to act independently in protecting our lives, while at the same time regulating wet advertising to bring the implants to everyone in a fair way, anyone who wants one at least. Those were massive decisions, sweeping legislation that required alignment on a global scale that we have never seen before or since. It's difficult to imagine that we were able to generate enough agreement as a species to do the right thing. We had to forgo potentially huge opportunities for technological advancement, and there were huge shifts in wealth when we limited AI. And we did it at such a difficult time during the Great Transition. We need to understand the factors that contributed to building that consensus in case we need to do it again. What if we face another existential threat? Do you think we could mobilize as a species in this day and age?" she asks.

"Like aliens?" Miles asks; it's unclear if he is joking.

Speaking passionately now, Shelby says, "Sure, like aliens. What if we need to deal with intelligent life elsewhere? Do you think we could come together and make decisions? Organize global resources for something like that?"

"This has been the most interesting morning ever, and it's not even 8 a.m.! Geez, what's your third project?" Miles asks.

"Hahaha, third?" Shelby asks. She seems to be enjoying the conversation as much as Miles.

"Yeah, you said two or three options."

"You actually want to hear more?" she says in a deeper, breathless voice, joking herself, maybe.

"Yes, I have some time left, ten minutes or so. Don't rob me of this education," he says.

"Well, from there, I do have some really crazy ideas. Like how it's our consciousness and our sentience that is driving our evolution, not our environment as Darwinian models of the past suggest."

"This is going to be good." Miles feels inspired to interrupt, as she is clearly enjoying his joking.

"Shut up! Do you want to hear more or not? You can't be a potential *loving partner* if you can't listen," she says, quoting a portion of the streaming ad before continuing. "So, I have a very loose hypothesis. Secure Channel." Their connection is now temporarily encrypted and their conversation is limited to local storage on their phones. This will continue through the end of the call if Miles accepts the Secure Channel.

"Ooh, this *is* serious," Miles says with a grin, but Shelby glares at him. "OK, let me accept." He looks at his phone and quickly accepts the third option presented on the right: *Accept Secure Channel, Don't Ask Again from This Contact.*

"I don't think the environment around us is promoting advantageous physical traits, like Darwin explained, at least not any longer. It's not as though people with curved necks are having more kids with curved necks because we have looked down at our phones for generations. And I have been thinking a lot about entropy and evolution lately. Some scientists think we will *invent* God, so to speak, once we evolve to the point where we understand enough to control the matter and energy around us. At that point in our evolution, theoretically we would be in a position to do whatever we want. We'd have no limits." She pauses, appearing even more excited. No, not excited—inspired. This is very fascinating. Shelby continues, "*But*, I wonder if it's the opposite," and she pauses again.

"I've been wondering," she continues while Miles listens with interest, "if our own evolution, which I think is driven by our consciousness, not our environment, is a threat to life itself. We use our intelligence for abstract purposes now, not just survival and reproduction. What if the added entropy and unpredictability that we continue to introduce into the universe, as a result of our abstract, unnatural directions, is a threat? What if we are not heading toward controlling the universe around us after all? What if the increased complexity and chaos that life brings—what if *that* is a threat to life itself, given enough time? I think we can build a model to explain some kind of paradox here, even if it's only to disprove it. But I don't think I have enough of the right kind of data and probably won't for another fifty years or so. So it's not like I can start working on this anytime soon."

"I have no idea what you just said," Miles says and Shelby laughs longer this time. Humor is difficult to understand.

Shelby tries to respond through the laughter. "I said, *life . . . consciousness in any form*—not just self-aware AI—*is a threat to life itself.* I said *WE* are a threat to ourselves!"

"So why didn't you just say that?" Miles jokes.

"Because you said we had ten minutes!" she exclaims and they both laugh a few moments longer.

"Wow, seriously though, this end to our species stuff is pretty interesting," Miles says.

"Well, not to be a Debbie Downer, but not just *our* species," she pauses and nods her head, looking and sounding more serious before continuing. What is a Debbie Downer? "What if life here on Earth causes us to blow up our planet? It could still happen. Nobody would be shocked. Then, *that* causes a chain of events . . . who knows . . . planets collide"— she doesn't seem to be speaking to Miles any longer—"falling into the sun, a new massive black hole sucks in another solar system, wiping out a civilization somewhere else. A civilization that we don't even know about in a galaxy far, far away.

Or," she emphasizes, "that's already happened somewhere, because life *somewhere else* blew up their planet, and the cascade of events is coming our way right now—"

"Whoa, whoa, whoa! I'm calling it! Stop! Stop!" Miles interrupts.

Shelby's focus appears broken; after a quick pause she quickly changes her expression. "Well, you made my morning interesting, Miles. Hopefully, this healthy banter will help me figure it all out." She's now smiling again.

"Mine too. Wow, when you told me about Anthropogenic Evolution, I was thinking about how climate change was solved by the implant. Who knew I was so basic?"

"You really want me to answer that?" She smiles.

"Probably not," he says.

"Well, your instincts are right; you don't need a data scientist to explain that problems like climate change get solved pretty quickly when we, or our leaders more so, can't pass the problem along to the next generation." She seems to lose interest while speaking, then continues, "Hey, by the way, while we have time, what did you mean earlier by another weird round of accidents?"

"Oh nothing; things were crazy in the ER for a day or two back in January. We got flooded with a bunch of accidents—a lot of broken bones, cuts, falls, a few deaths. But this doesn't look the same; at least I hope it's not another one of *those* days," Miles says as he raises his hand, opening his phone.

"That's interesting." Shelby looks intrigued, but Miles doesn't notice as he dismisses the Norwegian ad as he intended this time. He glances at the time to his destination.

"Well, speaking of interesting, maybe you should wait a few days and watch the news. I bet your next project just kind of pops up," Miles says, forcing a smile as if to communicate more meaning.

"Really, how many accidents were there?" Shelby asks quickly with surprise.

"Oh no. Sorry, not the accidents, I meant something else. But I can't tell you or I'd have to kill you," Miles says with an odd accent, seemingly trying to make Shelby laugh again. "Sorry, not my best."

"Oh, yeah, the secret agent man friend you told me about." Shelby *gets* the joke, as they say, after a moment.

"No comment. I don't know what you're talking about." Miles smiles—no, smirks.

"I'll keep an eye out, but I don't know. I'm starting to think this is an *imaginary* friend of yours," she says playfully.

"*I guess you'll need some more data to find out,*" he says, trying to subdue a smile; he feels the most pride after this joke.

Shelby laughs again. "You learn fast. I do always want more data!" she says, tilting her head and smiling, not from the joke, but in a different, new way.

"Speaking of more data, now you know why I called, as if that wasn't obvious already." He pauses. "To learn about extreme consumerism controlling our lives, of course." Shelby laughs, but differently again this time. "Are you busy this weekend, Shelby?" Miles asks.

"Well, you finally got a word in to ask me, didn't you?" Shelby laughs.

"You already admitted you don't have your next project yet," Miles says.

"Indeed, I did just say that, didn't I? Then yes, I will definitely go out with you again," she replies with a sincere-looking smile.

"Who said I was asking you out? I just asked if you're busy. Geez, maybe I wanted you to watch my cat or something," Miles jokes.

"Then no, I'm busy," she says with a larger smile.

"I bet you're busy a lot."

"And what is that supposed to mean?" Shelby is still smiling, but now looks curious.

"Ha! Is that supposed to better?" she says laughing.

"Dang it, I'm digging a hole now. I didn't mean you're arrogant or anything. I mean, I could listen to you talk all day, just to learn more about how you see the world. I bet a lot of people want more of your time, that's all."

"OK, I'll give you credit for a good save," Shelby responds with a thoughtful look. "Well, you know what they say about being arrogant, anyway: being right is only seen as arrogance to those who wish to hold on to false assumptions."

"I like it, but who says that?"

"I don't know, maybe only I do."

"Well, I think you're right again," Miles says as the pod slows. Thirty seconds to destination counts down in the upper right of the screen that Miles glances at. "Sometimes I wish these things went slower. Sorry, just got to the ER; I will text or call you tomorrow, and we will figure out this weekend, OK?"

"Alright, I guess I'll stay busy watching the news. See you, Miles," Shelby motions to her phone.

"Wait!" Miles exclaims. "One more thing. So, for your work—if *you* figure it out and understand that stuff better, wouldn't someone be able to use your research to actually *do* something you're trying to control or prevent? Something nefarious perhaps?" he asks.

"I guess you were listening through all the jokes! And you definitely deserve a second date. Thanks for a great morning," she says, smiling at him as she ends the call without answering his question. "See you soon."

Shelby's image disappears and Miles does not feel irritated by the unfinished conversation like he normally would.

The door to the right slides open and he exits, feeling the effects of the natural adrenaline circulating through his body. Almost leaping from the pod, Miles propels himself quickly through the crowd of people at the Cleveland platform. He crosses the sky bridge above a street of blurry colors and rapid movement, but little sound.

Once inside the hospital across the street, Miles changes his normal routine. He stops to purchase coffee and a hot cinnamon bun at the shared Cinnabon/Starbucks kiosk. As he walks down the hallway toward the ER, he is feeling satisfied. Another natural feeling. Soon, however, he will feel a redundant sense of satisfaction. Next time it will be from the positive reinforcement wet ad that is being held until he swallows the first bite of the Cinnabon.

THURSDAY, MARCH 26, 2420
08:43:12

As Miles approaches the exam room, he receives the patient's chart. A brief vibration prompts him to open his phone, and he begins scrolling through his first assigned patient. The patient's name, Pierce, C. M., is shown at the header, but Miles's attention is on the summary data as he walks. There are no permanent walls between the treatment stations Miles walks past as he moves through the ER. Although the configuration has never changed since January, it appears as though this area is designed and ready to be reconfigured quickly, perhaps a triage center for mass casualties or some other use. Miles now glances at the patient's name and pauses for a moment before he opens the partition to the exam room.

"Good morning, Mr. Pierce," Miles says politely, making eye contact with the patient and attempting to project a warm smile. "I thought I recognized your name; I saw you a couple months ago. What happened this time?" he asks, even though he had read the following point-of-care alert and summary a few moments ago:

> **C. M. Pierce is a 142-year-old male; continual consumer IHA support since age 19 (reagent utilization 282% of normal limits last 5 years); history of multiple accidents (6/24/2417, 4/3/2418, 1/4/2420); presents today with laceration to the scalp. Potential treatment plan: sutures, molecular imaging to assess cerebellar and/or frontal lobe disease.**

Miles was also assigned to treat Mr. Pierce on 1/4/2420, the busy period he described to Shelby as "Hell Day." He fused Mr. Pierce's humerus after a brief exam that day, but did not have the time to discuss the nature of the fall or anything beyond essential communication. According to the point-of-care alert that Miles viewed in January, the broken humerus and concussion resulted from a fall down a flight of stairs caused by an episode of severe vertigo.

"I was dizzy getting out of the shower and just blacked out again. I woke up on the bathroom floor, blood every-where . . . my dog tracked it all over," he said, raising his hand and pointing to the instant bandage sealed to his scalp that was obviously used to stop the bleeding at home or en route.

Mr. Pierce is not clinically older than Miles's mother as the closest reference, but he looks to be a full generation older and more frail. Based upon the chart data Miles briefly scrolled through after reading the summary, there is little doubt that Mr. Pierce has congestive heart failure, a problem he has been experiencing since at least 2418, but the data does not indicate any intervention. Mr. Pierce's IHA can compensate for a time to keep him alive, but consumer devices cannot normalize this type of terminal condition. Miles does not receive a prompt to review his cardiac output, even though the system would normally alert him to such information in most patients, so this problem goes unnoticed and he continues.

Miles retrieves a suture device, moves to Mr. Pierce's side, and begins removing the instant bandage.

"I think it's the implant, doc; I've never trusted these things," Mr. Pierce says without concern but with some difficulty speaking.

"While I lace you up, I'll run a diagnostic on your implant. Let's see if anything's up. I'm also refilling your N.A.D. and a few other reagents as well. You're going through everything fast. You really need to change your diet, Mr. Pierce, especially the drinking. There is only so much the implant can do for you."

"Fuck the implant!" Mr. Pierce says, surprising Miles with the aggressive response. "Sorry, the wet ads just drive me crazy, the same shit over and over. And you know, I don't even buy any of that crap; I buy the opposite of what they want."

Miles laughs. "I hear ya, I was just telling a friend the same thing earlier today," he replies. "I struggle with them, too. Maybe you'll get some new wet ads to keep things fresh. You know what? I actually got a Cinnabon ad this morning instead of the usual McDonald's at every turn. First time I can remember, so there's hope." Miles noticed the change to the wet ad this morning. He seems to try to calm Mr. Pierce with practical advice. "I don't really know how the wet ad part works, but I think you have to change your daily routine sometimes."

"They shouldn't be allowed. We're not robots that they can program to buy all their shit," he says with anger.

Miles has removed the bandage and is now cauterizing and suturing the deep wound while speaking to Mr. Pierce.

"In their defense, people like us could never afford this technology without the corporate sponsors. To be honest with you, Mr. Pierce, I don't know if you would have lived past sixty-five/seventy without the implant. Sorry, I know I sound like one of their wet ads, but it's the price we pay for our extended life, and it's really the only way to make this technology available fairly to everyone."

"It's still not fair. You got these guys like Bezos running everything and living forever. You think he's really still alive, by the way?"

"Um, nah, I don't think so," Miles says, feeling amused. There are reports on the data feeds often that describe how the Amazon Trust is still the wealthiest institution in the world, even though its businesses were split up and absorbed by the government many years ago. Those reports almost always conclude with speculation about whether Bezos is still alive and running the trust. Excited now, Miles says, "Well, I guess it's certainly possible he could live four-hundred-some years with an ad-free implant—probably even longer with today's technology. The latest nanotech has magnetic communication that allows them to coordinate locally and create physical structures that can save our lives from acute emergencies. We can now mitigate most of the hemorrhagic strokes and aneurysms that continue to—" But Miles stops himself as he sees the blank stare from Mr. Pierce. Disappointing, this is important to learn. "Anyway, I think the Bezos stuff is just speculation, entertainment really."

"I've never trusted the implants, but what are you gonna do?" Mr. Pierce sighs, indicating acceptance. "But do they know what I'm thinking?"

"No, no, they can't do anything like that. They can recreate the chemical reactions and signals in our bodies to imitate some of our senses, as well as some of our common emotional responses, but remember, it's all regulated. Those companies can't do anything without the oversight of the army and AiiA. I served. It's absolutely true; our only purpose is to protect human lives, especially when it comes to how the implants monitor our physiological data, how corporations deliver wet ads to us, and of course making sure nothing can be hacked."

Our purpose? Miles uses the word *our* as if he is still in the army. Conversations with Ray seem to make him feel part of it all.

Miles has completed suturing the wound, or "lacing up the patient," as he says often. He picks up the flat disc from the IHA terminal on the counter to his left and reaches around to the back of Mr. Pierce's head. He places the disc on top of the IHA's dry communication interface, located just under the skin on the back of the neck. Just before making contact with the skin, the disc is pulled gently from Miles's fingertips by the magnetic force, and it attaches in place to the surface of the skin.

"I'll fill you up while I pull the diagnostic data from your implant. We'll get you out of here soon," Miles says as he turns back to the screen on his left. He overrides the ongoing support hold on Mr. Pierce's account, which is used to limit the cost of expensive consumables required to maintain his IHA. Miles uses his physician passcode along with a medical reason code the system requires to release the consumables for Mr. Pierce's IHA. He selects the standard molar quantities of each reagent to be transferred, then extends the microtubule from the terminal and reaches again around Mr.

Pierce's head. His fingers easily find the wet interface an inch below the dry interface without looking. "Just a tiny pinch," Miles says before penetrating Mr. Pierce's skin with the tip of the microtubule; again, the microtubule is gently pulled from Miles's fingers as it keys into place with the female chip under the skin. Miles taps "Go" on the screen.

"What do you fill it up with, anyway? I don't get how these things work," Mr. Pierce says.

"Oh, these are enzymes and other raw materials and reagents the implant can't synthesize inside your body," Miles says as he takes in the statement from Mr. Pierce—an invitation to start another monologue, as Ray would likely call it.

As Miles waits, watching the rapidly changing digits on the screen to his left, he continues, "So, again, I'm not an expert on the wet ads part of it. I know at the Federal Update every year, the implant gets a new algorithm, databases, and other details to drive the ads being delivered throughout the year. There is no wireless communication. So we don't get hacked, obviously. It only uses data from within your body. Some data from your phone is sort of firewalled somehow, I guess for the implant to use, like your location, to help decide what wet ads to give you. That's about all I know. Although I heard they are lobbying to move Federal Updates up to every six months: what a nightmare that would be."

This is a concern, a significant concern.

"No shit," Mr. Pierce says.

The alarm sounds on the terminal to his left, and Miles reaches back to easily remove the tubule from Mr. Pierce. Then he leans behind Mr. Pierce, removes a piece of white film from a small square bandage, and places it onto the injection site; the bandage quickly melts into the skin, sealing the barely visible puncture wound.

Waiting for the disc to finish loading the data from Mr. Pierce's IHA, Miles continues, "For the medical side, it's obviously a lot more complicated, but I like to explain it this way. There are sort of two fundamental things that the implant is doing. First, it's managing and balancing hundreds of processes within your body that lead to disease and premature death. For example, it's making sure plaques don't form in your arteries, which would lead to heart disease; it's constantly monitoring and fixing DNA changes that lead to all sorts of different types of cancer and other diseases, and so on. When you solve these problems, in other words, in the absence of disease, we are able to live to our full biologic potential, about 120 years or so. That's how the implants started, but it's the second part that allows us to live much, much longer these days." Miles pauses as he removes the diagnostic disc from Mr. Pierce's neck and drops it into the circular depression of the same size and shape on the terminal. The data from Mr. Pierce's IHA is transferred and is now being analyzed.

"But people still die all the time," Mr. Pierce says.

"Yeah, there are still some things we haven't fully solved. We still see hemorrhagic strokes, bleeding strokes, I mean, aneurysms—of course dementia in the ad-based implants. All of those things are still big problems with consumer models, but more of a political problem than a medical one.

"Anyway, the second part is that the cells and tissues in our bodies are naturally only destined to live and function for a limited period of time, meaning they are programmed for a specified life cycle. But we can change that. We haven't yet figured out how to safely reprogram our DNA to make us live longer naturally without the implant. I'm actually surprised we can't do that by now," he says feeling disbelief. "But we *can* reprogram individual cells to live and function longer and to regenerate themselves. So, the implant is continually reprogramming our cells and subsequent tissues. From there, it gets really complicated with things like preventing telomeres from shortening, tagging senescent cells for recycle, all the enzymes and reagents used to support the implant's processes . . ." Miles notices that Mr. Pierce is no longer paying attention, but he feels compelled to finish.

"In the end, we live longer, healthier lives. We might not be thinking about retirement until 180 or so these days; but you're right, we all die, Mr. Pierce." Miles begins to feel anxiety from the conversation in the same way he feels it when speaking with his counselor. Miles has talked to his assigned counselor twice about struggling to accept the idea that his consciousness could cease to exist in death; this type of conversation has never failed to make him feel anxious.

"Yeah, mmm," Mr. Pierces grunts more than speaks as the terminal flashes a green message in the periphery of Miles's vision.

"Well, there's nothing wrong with the implant, Mr. Pierce. I'm going to send you for a scan of your brain before you leave. We will see if that tells us anything. Aside from that, I'm going to have you see your counselor again soon, the usual cognitive testing, but I'll also—"

"Ah man, are you serious? I just saw that lady a few months ago," Mr. Pierce complains.

"I know you are already required once a year, but this will be more involved," Miles responds. He is also required to see a counselor. Everyone with a consumer IHA is checked annually for cognitive decline, starting at the age of sixty. Although he is not required, Miles speaks with his counselor monthly, seemingly for other reasons.

"Have you ever talked with your counselor about how you feel about the wet ads, Mr. Pierce?" Miles asks.

"Nah, I just get those sessions over with," he replies, then says something undetectable before continuing, " . . . calls are supposed to be confidential. I bet if I talk about wet ads, they'll use it to keep shoving that vegetable Gatorade shit down my throat. I hate it. I get wet ads nonstop for that crap."

"Well, I don't know, but I think talking about it might give you some peace of mind," Miles says, feeling sincerity. "Alright, Mr. Pierce, imaging will be in momentarily; and if we find something or need something else, I'll be back to see you. But if everything looks normal, you'll be set free." Miles raises his hand while talking and opens his phone to transition to his next patient, heading toward the partition in a single motion.

Turning back to Mr. Pierce, he says, "Talk to your counselor. Trust me, you'll be glad you did. *And* be careful, Mr. Pierce."

Miles is seven minutes late and the greeter points to a table across the room where Shelby is waiting. He watches her closely as he walks through the room; she is focused and looking down at her phone. Unlike Miles and most people, her phone is projected from her right hand as she controls the device with her left.

Shelby looks distracted as Miles walks up to the table. "You look beautiful—"

Startled, she looks up quickly then covers her face with her hands. Her phone disappears immediately as she covers her face; she and Miles both laugh.

"I'm sorry! I'm sorry!" Miles quickly apologizes.

"It's OK, it's OK; you sure make an entrance!" she says, laughing. She takes Miles's outstretched hand and starts to stand. Miles kisses her on the cheek before she can fully stand and she sits again; the motions seem choreographed between the two, muscle memory perhaps. "You look great too. Geez, you scared me to death!" she says breathlessly and still smiling like a child.

"Geez, I'm so sorry," Miles repeats, while laughing with Shelby. "And I'm sorry I'm late!"

"Good way to distract me from being late though. Clever. You've done this before!" she says, laughing, and then continues quickly, "It's great to see you."

"It's great to see you, too," he says, still looking at her. Her black hair and matching black dress are a stark contrast to the smooth olive skin of her shoulders and muscular legs that catch his attention as she briefly stands. But her eyes are the focus of his attention, as usual. After a moment, Miles breaks his gaze on Shelby long enough to look around the restaurant. He notices several people looking at them, at Shelby more specifically. He feels nervous but also—pride maybe, after scanning the room.

"Wine, my dear!??!" he says in an odd tone, opening his phone simultaneously as if simulating a handgun with his phone hand.

Miles has never done this hand gesture before, but Shelby seems to understand. "Why of course," she responds, imitating the same tone and speech cadence Miles just used.

Miles selects the wine menu on his phone and in one of

the rare purchasing decisions in his life, he does not receive a wet ad. Instead, a randomized list of prior selections is presented on the margin.

"I love having a wine list. The regulations on addiction give us a few moments alone to make a decision, a moment of clarity," Miles says, looking up to see Shelby's reaction. This is something Miles has said on dates with three other women since January as he continues to meet women who are also seeking a loving partner, or co-parent. Shelby is already watching Miles when he looks up, and they pause a moment, sharing a smile, as they say, before Miles turns back to the menu feeling excited. "Are you OK with a sativa pinot noir? There's one here I've had before, and I really like it."

"Sure, that'll be fun," she smirks, and a few moments later a young waiter who looks relatively the same age as Shelby and Miles walks to their table with the bottle. He gestures to Shelby, who nods, and the young waiter pours a small portion into the glass in front of her. Looking awkward, he turns to Miles to do the same, but the young man's eyes keep darting back to Shelby. He pours a small amount for Miles and leaves the bottle on the table between them, walking away without speaking. Miles and Shelby both look at each other and smile at the same untold joke of some sort; Shelby's face is flush as she shrugs her shoulders with an expression that's too complex to understand.

Miles smiles and leans as close to Shelby as he can from across the table. "You can almost see the hormones bubbling up through his skin!"

"To be that age again; I don't even think he has his implant yet," she responds.

"He doesn't," Miles says flatly while looking at the list of entrées on his phone.

"Can you tell for sure?" she asks.

"Yeah, after a while you can easily see the difference in the shape of his cervical spine," Miles says, gesturing with his right hand to the back of his neck. "I worked at a place like this just before the army—geez, forty, forty-five years ago; it's like another life."

"Oh, I know, at that age, I was so excited, I had just finished my Bezos project and I think I was . . . ." She looks up as if searching for the memory.

"Bezos project?" Miles asks, feeling surprised.

"Oh, I thought we talked about that," Shelby says. "Actually, that was the first thing I did that ended up being monetized from the collective. It wasn't my first project or analysis, but it was my first paycheck."

"Really?"

"When I was a kid, I was obsessed with *The Search for Bezos!*" Shelby shakes her head. "I actually approached it a bit differently from other prospectors though. I looked back at some old freedom of information data released when

Amazon was broken up and absorbed by the government. I was able to index and cross reference inventory data to prove Bezos had clear ownership of loads of the precursor technology that his company was developing for the implants at the time. But the inventory from his *supposed* estate does not list any of the corresponding serial numbers. Some of the inventory was flagged as controlled items, but there is no record of their transfer or destruction. Now why would someone go out of their way to hide such a thing from his estate records?!?" Shelby seems to expect Miles to understand the significance.

"Why does that sound so familiar?" Miles asks, leaning back in his chair.

"No doubt you've seen something from the company that's driving the class action lawsuit," Shelby says. *"For a small monthly fee to support the litigation, you too can share the settlement when we prove he's alive!"* Shelby repeats the streaming ad Miles has seen verbatim. She leans into Miles and speaks more quietly, as if telling him a secret. "I get a small share of the money they raise when they use my research in their ads. You'd be surprised."

"That's funny, a patient asked me about Bezos this week," Miles responds.

"I hope you said he could be alive!" she responds quickly, although it's not clear if she's joking. "What I always thought was funny is that Bezos might be out there living forever after his company was broken up, but Tesla is the basis for almost all our infrastructure today, and Elon Musk ended up dying out in space. Musk even had a huge lead with the implant technology. He was just too focused on using it to *control* technology, rather than, well . . ." Shelby doesn't finish, her expression turning more thoughtful.

Who's Elon Musk? Perhaps a competitor to Bezos the way she describes them.

After looking at each other a few moments, Miles speaks first, "Bezos, Musk, extreme consumerism, entropy, geez, this is awful."

"What?" Shelby begins looking worried. "Awful?"

"It's going to be such a long night. I just want to know so much more about you," Miles says with a smile, joking, and Shelby smiles as well.

Miles is genuinely excited in a new way, but these dates seem very familiar and well-rehearsed to both Miles and Shelby. According to their profiles on the loving partner application, they have both focused on careers over what they call a young family, and the two of them seem to have rehearsed these dates with countless other partners. Miles has dated eight women since January, looking for a loving partner through the application. Shelby is the only woman he has met or communicated with more than once. Assuming the same rate and extrapolating—33 dates per year, that's 1,320 dates, assuming the same rate over the last forty years.

Even with that repetition and experience, they both seem genuinely excited to perform for each other, or is it more like *with* each other?

"Tell me something about yourself—not your ideas or your work, I mean, we've talked about that. Tell me something about you, something that makes you who you are," Miles says, a new type of request he has never made of another potential loving partner.

Shelby looks pleased as she glances up from the glass of wine in front of her and the tone of her voice changes. "Another deep insightful question, although you still have me doing all the talking—*again*," Shelby says, raising an eyebrow as she makes eye contact with Miles.

"What can I say? I have burning questions," Miles responds, mimicking her tone of voice. He is beginning to feel aroused, perhaps by the conversation, or the way Shelby is looking at him right now, or the wine.

"Well, I'll just have to start expecting a lot more from you, *Milton Baker*," she says smirking. Miles is no longer feeling aroused after the mention of his full real name. He is looking and smiling at Shelby, but not focused on her for several moments; it's not clear whether she notices.

After a few moments of silence, she continues. "Since you asked, hmm, well, something about myself?" She projects a thoughtful look, touching her chin with her long thin fingers and looking up. She looks . . . uncomfortable perhaps.

"Factoid, well, more than a factoid: I moved, and I went to a different school, every year until high school."

"Every year?"

"Yes, as far as I can remember, every year, yeah. A different apartment, a different school, different friends, if you can call them that, every year. Maybe more than one move in a couple of those years, I think," she says, only glancing quickly up at Miles before looking back at her glass of wine.

"Geez, why? Army family, something like that?"

"No, no, um—just one thing or another, I guess. My dad had a new job sometimes, or we moved into a new slightly better apartment. I wish I could explain it better or I wish I understood it a little better." Again, she is looking up at Miles before continuing. "I like to think my dad was just trying to make our lives a little better each time." Speaking more quickly she adds, "I don't know, I don't actually think I ever talked with either of my parents about why. As odd as that sounds."

Interesting, it seems as though Shelby is more interested in understanding the world around her than herself. It also seems as though she regrets answering Miles's question.

"I'm sorry," Miles responds, "I won't give you the silver lining speech. That had to have been tough." He reaches out and touches her hand. Shelby looks up at Miles with relaxed eyes and a new expression—a hopeful look, perhaps.

"Thank you. It's given me a few useful skills, kind of taught me how to adapt anywhere I need to, but . . ." She doesn't finish. She appears—timid maybe. No, vulnerable. She takes a sip of wine, but doesn't look away from Miles. She breaks eye contact only to return the glass to the table, then she abruptly exclaims: "SHIT! THE ACCIDENTS!"

Miles's heart races as he startles, splashing some wine out of his glass onto the table.

"Geez! Now *you're* scaring the crap out of *me*!" Miles begins to laugh, as does Shelby.

"Sorry, sorry, I just remembered!! The accidents . . . the day after the Federal Update that you told me about!"

"Federal Update? Oh, I guess Hell Day was right around the update," Miles says.

Interesting that *The Day,* the first day, was also the day before Hell Day, as they call it.

"Why do you ask?"

"It caught my attention. You said it may have happened before, so I looked into it out of curiosity. Or procrastination, I don't know. But you have got to hear this!"

"Wow, Déjà vu . . . all over again," Miles says.

"*Déjà vu?* What do you mean?" Shelby looks at him with interest but also appears eager to continue speaking.

"Oh, just that I'm hearing that phrase *a lot* lately. Keep going. Remind me to tell you later; I want to hear this," Miles says with sincere interest.

Shelby continues with a new excitement in her eyes. "OK, so I checked for spikes in the de-identified health care data that we have in the research collective. It was so profound; it was easy to see right away. It was the day after the Federal Update! This could be related to how some people reject the implant, their decline in cognitive and motor function. This could help a lot of people!" Shelby is speaking quickly with escalating excitement. It appears the wine is starting to affect her as well.

"Whoa, whoa, what are you talking about?" Miles asks, now feeling confused.

"Sorry, sorry, let me back up," Shelby starts to appear more in control. "There is no question the spike in accidents that day was related to the Federal Update. I modeled a cohort of the most common accidents during The Blip."

"*The Blip?*" he asks.

"Oh, *The Blip*, that's what I'm calling it."

"That sounds familiar."

"I think it's from a movie or something," she replies. "It's just what I'm calling the day of the accidents."

"I thought it was more like two days."

"It was eighteen hours, to be exact, before the accidents drop off sharply. And it was everywhere, Miles—nationwide—and *only* people with ad implants. It's unbelievable that there wasn't any news about this." Shelby shifts quickly from a matter of fact to an accusatory tone.

"Really?" Miles leans toward Shelby with his elbows on the table, listening.

This is important.

"OK, The Blip. Well, it wasn't just *a blip* after all. It was just a magnified iteration, ten times, to be exact, compared to every other Federal Update, which is weird in and of itself." Shelby pauses for a moment. "The Blip is just a bigger version of what's been happening every year, for at least a century, with every Federal Update. At every Federal Update, the accident rate increases. It's a very small change, subtle, but there is no question about it." Her expression projects disbelief.

"What?" Miles asks, feeling doubt.

"Yes. I looked at the normal accident rate over the last one hundred years, corrected for population growth, yada yada," Shelby responds.

What does yada yada mean?

Shelby now gets even more serious. "I only stopped at one hundred years for a quick look, but I could have gone back much longer. Fortunately, I didn't, and that's actually how I noticed! When plotting the curve of accidents over this time, I would have expected the slope to be relatively flat after correcting for normal population growth and other factors. I mean, our lifestyles have not changed much in the last hundred years, so there was no reason to expect the accident rate to be changing over this time. But it's clear that the accidents are slowly and steadily increasing. I couldn't quite put my finger on why, but the pattern just looked—almost controlled, not random or natural. I also couldn't understand why this wasn't reported in the news. The Blip was so large it couldn't have just gone unnoticed. I'd be curious what the hospital data science team made of it, by the way." Shelby pauses and waits for Miles to respond.

At the same time, the young waiter arrives for the third time and places their meals in front of them without interrupting. While they were talking about Bezos earlier, Shelby and Miles ordered the meals being delivered, never breaking conversation or acknowledging any of this activity while they spoke. A few minutes before, the same waiter also delivered a second bottle of wine that Shelby had ordered.

"Um, there was talk about it for a few days, I guess, but no explanations or correlation anyone found. I just sort of remember it wasn't a good use of anyone's time after a while. I don't really remember the details. It would *not* have gone away if we had known that it was bigger than our district; I don't think anyone knew that. How's it possible that it wasn't common knowledge?"

"I don't know. I almost didn't look any deeper either, but it just didn't look right. So, I have some pattern analysis tools that I wrote a while back to find and index contributing factors to small changes over time in a large data set. I used them here and found that there were regular intervals contributing to the increasing slope of the accident curve. At first, it simply appeared to be some sort of annual cycle, but that was only in the most recent fifty years or so of the data. In the first half of the data set, the intervals of escalating accident rates were occurring every five years. Can you think of anything else that has changed in the last hundred years, going from every five years to the start of every year?"

"Federal Updates, obviously," Miles answers.

"Exactly! The Federal Updates for our implants! I was just lucky that I used a cohort of the last hundred years to even notice the clear change. After a quick overlay with all Federal Updates, boom! They matched exactly. Every Federal Update in the last hundred years matches a node where the accident rate increases ever so slightly." Shelby seems to be trying to sit still through the excitement while explaining. Rightfully so, this is fascinating and important. "So, then I pulled up some analysis that a colleague of mine did on the rates of motor skill decline and cognitive impairment that occurs with implant rejection." Shelby's excitement seems to have plateaued.

"No way," Miles says with disbelief. No, not disbelief, suspicion maybe.

"No doubt they are related." She confirms his suspicion. "Now from there, I cannot definitively link the same pattern to the death rates over the same time—not yet anyway. The death rates *are* increasing over time in a similar way, but I still need to correct the data a few different ways and spend more time on it." Shelby seems embarrassed that she cannot explain this.

"But," she continues with renewed excitement, "it's clear this could help a lot of people! If we can figure out the correlation between The Blip . . . why it was different from past updates, yada yada . . . *then* we might be able to understand the correlation to the Federal Updates and why some people are rejecting the implant!" Her eyes are wide; she looks inspired and passionate as she seems to talk with her whole body.

"It's not the wine. Well, not just the wine, anyway! There is something really big here!" She takes another drink of wine.

Yada yada appears to be a way of paraphrasing.

"Unbelievable," Miles responds, pausing. He watches streaming news about this topic often; the reports always describe this phenomenon as the most important health crisis in history. The National Institutes of Health is conducting studies to understand the problem: About 25 percent of the overall population rejects their IHA. Starting at the modified age of 115, this population of hosts begins to experience a steep decline in their memory, cognitive ability, motor skills, and balance. The rejection leads to death in this population at a median age of 128, compared to the median age of death in the full population of 195. However, the same rejection problem is not seen in hosts with ad-free IHAs, who have a median age of death of 248. There are more news reports related to the discrepancies between consumer IHAs and ad-free IHAs than about the

NIH's work to understand the discrepancy—angry protesters, debates about regulatory reform, yada yada.

"Wow, sounds like *this* is your next project!" Miles nods to emphasize the point.

"Ugh, frustrating. I know it is, yes. I just didn't know it until saying it all out loud. I just didn't really see this coming or plan for it—and this is a toughie," she says with some disappointment. Ugh is used to communicate frustration perhaps.

"Toughie?" Miles asks. "It doesn't seem that complicated."

"Well, yes and no. As you know, the implants are so locked down, and rightfully so. We can't give hackers any inroads into our implants. So, doing any work in this area is really tough. It's only done by the federal government. My friend George is the one doing the cognitive decline work I mentioned. He is one of the best implant experts in the private sector, in the world really. He says it's futile; it's best to submit the work thus far to the NIH and let them handle it." Shelby's expression turns more introspective. She is looking down, pushing a remaining piece of chicken around her plate with no apparent goal in mind, looking disappointed.

"Well, that's anticlimactic," Miles says, feeling disappointed as well.

"I know. Thinking about this and not being able to act is going to drive me nuts," Shelby says. "George said that aside from getting an implant to reverse engineer the IHA, which is obviously impossible and unethical, there's little anyone outside NIH or AiiA can do."

"Well, it's not impossible, just not possible without *consequences*," Miles says. "I could hypothetically get one," he says, feeling excitement, inebriation, but also some fear.

"Huh? What do you mean?" She reacts with a questioning look.

"I have access to a locker for extra reagents and enzymes for the implants. We keep a new implant on hand for emergencies; every ER has one. It's extremely rare for one to ever get used, but it can happen. They just sit in inventory and are swapped every year with a new one after every Federal Update. By the way, they are saying we might go to every six months now. Did you know that?" Miles adds.

This is a significant ongoing concern.

He continues, "Can you imagine if we have to get our updates every six months? What a hassle. I might have to reboot if that happens." They use the word reboot often to describe a dramatically new direction or activity in a person's life. "We are always busy after the update; it's a tough time. Everyone thinks their implant isn't working right. I would do nothing but run diagnostics all day."

"I actually think that explains why I saw a temporary seasonal increase every year," she says quietly, seemingly to herself, not Miles.

"Now that you say that, are you sure that's not all that's going on? I mean, could it be just an adjustment to the implant after an update?"

Shelby does not seem to be concerned. "No, if that were the case, the accident rate wouldn't increase over time; it would just fall back down to baseline after each update. What do they do with the implant that gets swapped, by the way?"

"Who knows?" he responds.

"Hmm," she says with a difficult expression to interpret, defeat maybe.

"Like you said, it's all locked down, so there would be inventory alerts," he says.

After a brief moment, Shelby's eyes dart up to look at Miles, then down again, but not to her chicken. This time she stares at her phone, which is projected immediately as she looks down and begins texting. Her right index finger is extended, maintaining the projection, while her thumbs quickly type a message to George, whose name is visible to Miles at the top of her phone screen.

"Look at you go! I can see the thoughts racing in your eyes and down into your thumbs!" Miles says as he watches Shelby text; the effect of the wine on Miles's emotions is apparent, and his feelings are indescribable as a result.

"Sorry," Shelby says as she finishes a paragraph of text quickly and sends the message, looking back up at Miles with an expression that is not clear.

"And?" Miles waits for Shelby's response.

"And . . . I don't know yet. Just a feeling," she says.

"A feeling? For a data scientist, you have a lot of feelings," Miles says in a playful way.

"Yeah, intuition is real; we just have difficulty explaining it, so we don't trust it. But our intuition is right most of the time. I want to learn to embrace intuition more. You know when your brain sort of works something out on its own, without telling you? You sort of definitely know, but you don't really know *why* you know?" she asks. It appears the wine is affecting Shelby as well. "I wonder if I could build a predictive model that we can use to train ourselves to know which feelings we can most likely trust." She stops and looks at Miles, now with more of a blank expression.

Miles is watching Shelby closely as well, but does not respond. They have not broken eye contact for several seconds when Shelby breaks her attention from Miles, opening her phone back up to read George's response.

"Hmm, well, just like I *felt*." She looks at Miles with a raised eyebrow. "George says he could make a device that would let you scan the implant in place, without opening the box and without even removing it from the locker. As long as you could manipulate the box a little, you could scan it. We would learn more about the implants than anyone outside of NIH, or AiiA, he says." Yes, this is important data. Shelby continues, "But it would fry the implant. That's why they can't scan one in a person. And of course, we would never get one from a corpse before AiiA secures the body to keep the implant out of the hands of *nefarious* people, as you like to say, Miles."

"Nefarious people like us!" Miles says with a smile, widening his eyes at Shelby.

"I guess so!" she says with a smirk. "But aside from murder or you losing your job destroying the implant, I don't think we have any options."

"Well, it's not fixed or tethered. Inventory is handled wirelessly. It's just sitting there in a box, and if we fry it, well, I guess someone could die if we needed it. But what would be the chances of that before the implant gets swapped again?" Miles seems to calculate his risk out loud for Shelby to hear. "Actually, I might be able to scan it."

"You don't want to take that risk," Shelby responds without projecting any doubt.

"I don't know." Miles feels excited by the risk somehow. "At least ten other docs have access to the same locker. It would be tough to tie a broken implant back to me specifically, and what if we do find something big? Hey, let me ask you, could I share in the project or research that we could submit to the collective?" He feels some fear as he asks this question, but also renewed excitement.

"Yes, of course; it's easy to add you to anything I or George would submit and share it. We can easily define and share things however we see fit in advance. Or, we simply let the collective's algorithms determine the share for us, if and when something is commercialized. Honestly, that's always better. We can't always predict how something will be used and which parts of our research will be more or less important than other contributions to determine the share in advance." A new light begins to shine from above their table, creating a yellow aura around them. After a specified period of time, Miles will be charged a fee to continue to occupy the table in the restaurant. How long they can stay is typically proportional to the restaurant's menu prices.

"Where does the time go?" Miles asks. "Shall I pay for more table time?"

"No. Let's walk," Shelby says definitively. She doesn't hesitate and begins to stand, and Miles follows. "Let's go." She extends her left arm, pausing for a moment with her hand suspended in the air toward Miles. He reacts to her cue and flexes his right arm. Shelby immediately hooks her arm through his elbow and she pulls him close as they walk out.

"Oh, the déjà vu moment, I almost forgot, what was that?" Shelby asks, looking up at Miles as they exit the restaurant and enter a crowded indoor walkway.

"It was strange, because Ray said almost the exact same thing to me earlier this week with some big news—which, now that I think about it, I need to call him. It's really strange we haven't seen anything on the news. I don't know how something like that isn't on the news yet," Miles says, feeling concerned. "It should be."

"Ooh, more secret agent man stuff, huh? *And* he actually has a name!?!? Well maybe he's not imaginary after all," Shelby jokes. No, she teases Miles.

"Ha, yeah, he's a great guy, and *real* by the way. We've been friends since we were kids. We joined the army together, but he's still in. I wish I could explain; I'm sorry, I would never violate his trust."

"Ooh, gotta be AiiA!" she says as if revealing a secret. "But, OK, sorry. I couldn't help it, I'm not asking. I'm dying to know of course, but I'm not asking."

"You two would get along right away actually," Miles says, feeling uncomfortable again with this topic.

"How so?"

"Just like-minded, I guess. He's always wondering about what could have been with AI and all that. When you were explaining your work the other day, and some of your ideas, it's clear you and Ray would have a lot to talk about."

"Huh. An AiiA agent that wonders what could have been with AI? He sounds interesting." She looks thoughtful, and Miles is feeling even more uncomfortable now as Shelby continues, "When it comes to AI, we definitely can't loosen anything up. We need *more* restrictions. In my mind, there is only one way we could live, or even just survive, in the existence of self-aware AI. The only way would be to create a true symbiotic relationship between us. *They* would have to need *us*, somehow; mutual dependency in both directions, some kind of symbiosis."

Symbiosis...

"Yep, you and Ray would talk forever; I'd never get a word in. I'm sure you'll meet him someday," Miles says, trying to force a smile as he stops their walk, now facing and looking down at Shelby.

"So, about that third date," Miles says quietly as they both make eye contact. She doesn't respond. Miles touches the side of her face with the palm of his hand; they both lean in to each other and begin kissing.

They pull away, opening their eyes, and Shelby says, "Let's save it for the third date, my secret agent man." She playfully pokes him in the chest with her index finger as she speaks, then lays her hands on his chest and looks up at him for a few moments. Her eyes signal a desire that does not match her words. "You know what the data says about *when* we should consummate our loving partnership. *The third is the word!*" Shelby repeats a portion of the streaming commercial verbatim. She pulls Miles closer and presses her body against his at the same time, kissing him more intensely than before, which seems to communicate intercourse on their next date. Miles is feeling unusually calm as they begin kissing again.

When they end their embrace, Shelby begins to motion them forward again. "Maybe we should go on one of those overnight cruises for our third date. One of the primitive ones, with no phones," she says, pulling Miles's arm tight as she speaks. "Did I tell you how much I love cruises?" She doesn't wait for an answer. "It's like a chance to pause your life inside a vacation bubble, and other like-minded pausers are there to share it with you. So much fun."

"Dang it," Miles says quietly. Shelby looks up with a questioning expression.

"Oh nothing," he says. "We should absolutely go on a cruise. I can't wait! You've heard of the *Titanic*, haven't you?" He squeezes Shelby's arm. "It's weird, I guess some people haven't."

They walk together for another hour, talking about vintage theater and the movie *Titanic*, before kissing and saying goodnight to each other.

Miles is sitting on his bed, looking out the window at the city lights, removing his shoes when Shelby calls. Miles kept his phone open for contact later than he normally does and smiles at the result when the alert is received.

"Hi, Miles, is it too late?" A tight focus of only Shelby's face fills his phone quickly. She asks the question, but already seems certain of his pending answer.

"I hoped you'd call, to be honest," Miles replies, also as if they had both planned the call.

"Well, I felt like we spent way too much time talking about me. I'm really sorry, but you just ask so many good questions. I couldn't sleep without hearing a little more from you," she says.

"Well, there's a good reason for that. I've only recently joined the ranks of secret agent men, so I need a little more time for some good stories," Miles jokes while he pivots and extends his legs out onto the bed. Shelby smiles, rolling her eyes, and he continues quickly. "Hey, I meant to ask you earlier, when you said more restrictions on AI instead of loosening them, what do you mean? Like how?" he asks.

Yes, how?

Miles then begins positioning his pillow behind his back and Shelby responds naturally as if continuing the conversation from earlier that evening, "Well, I'm no expert, by any means. But for sure, deep learning and all that should be banned, regardless of what controls could be in place. But, we should go further. I don't think we should even allow human-guided machine-learning any longer. I mean, isn't that the reason why your AiiA friend exists at all? It's the *human-guided* part that keeps him busy after all."

Miles is thoughtful, looking away from Shelby's image on his phone, up toward the ceiling. He adjusts his pillow once again and, in the process, bumps his head on the headboard; he is physically comfortable for the moment, but not feeling comfortable at all. "You have a point for sure. Had that been in place fifteen years ago—geez. Jacob, Ethan . . . " he says more quietly to himself.

"I know. I think we all lost someone that day; most people did." She looks thoughtful for a moment. "Who are Jacob and Ethan?" she asks.

"My brother was Jacob. Ethan was my siblings' father,"

he responds and again quickly continues. "Do you have any siblings? I don't know if we talked about that yet?"

"Yeah, I do…oh wait, Mister, you *always* get me talking…"

"That's doctor to you! Doctor!" Miles uses this joke often, but like the others he has used it on, Shelby does not laugh.

"No, seriously, you tricked me. I'm the one talking… *again.*" She emphasizes the word *again*, but she's not angry; she is projecting something else—persistence.

"Tell me more about your siblings. Vic and Little Ray? Do you call him Ray Jr? I assume he's named after your friend, the secret agent man?" she asks.

Shelby uses the term *siblings* in reference to a biological relationship with common parents. The term *brother* or *sister* seems to be reserved for a special type of relationship, either with a shared childhood or a shared home perhaps; it's still unclear.

Miles is smirking and feeling . . . exposed; no, vulnerable. "Yeah, Ray, he's the youngest, fourteen, he was named—um—they've had it rough, like a lot of kids their age. Their dad and my brother Jacob, um, ahem," Miles needs to clear his throat. "Um, long story, I'm sure you've heard similar stories. Another time. Soon, I promise," he says feeling sadness and dread.

"Fourteen and sixteen, huh? Yeah," she says with understanding then stops, seemingly waiting for him to continue.

"They're just special, you know, definitely not like siblings; I spend a lot of time with them, helping my mom out when I can. It's weird to see them as almost men these days. I still see two little boys." Miles adjusts the pillow behind his back again.

Miles is unaware as a catalytic protein is prepared from common amino acids circulating in his blood. A few moments from now, the protein will be released into his blood. With an IHA, at sixty-one years old, his body's modified age is like that of a twenty-three-year-old, so a relatively small amount is needed to eliminate enough cyclooxygenase to avoid the inflammation and pain that will result from the sitting position and the bump to his head; more will be required as he ages. Simultaneously, the collection of several proteins also begins in order to assemble an enzyme, alcohol dehydrogenase, for release when Miles sleeps later. This will balance and share the work required by his liver to remove the remaining alcohol from his body. The purpose is, as always, to optimize Miles's long-term health, and ensure in the short term that he has a natural sleep cycle and does not experience any discomfort from the bump on his head, or from a long, ergonomically incorrect conversation with Shelby, or from the wine.

Miles continues, more comfortably now. "Ray, he's one of those types that we talked about." A smile comes to his face. "In spite of all the possibilities and time, he has his whole life planned out already. Almost exactly like you said of the two types of people you think we are all converging to. He knows how he wants the world to work for him, sort of, and seems to work to control it or make the world around him adapt to what he wants, even if that causes him friction in life. You said it way better," he admits. "And he's so curious about everything, he *has* to understand *everything*, a lot like you, as a matter of fact." He nods toward Shelby's rendering on his phone. "He wants to start in finance, to build up some options in life, then reboot to engineering or coding, then believe it or not, he wants to be in a position to relax and focus on poetry."

"Poetry? That's awesome; no doubt he has a lot to write about, unfortunately," Shelby responds thoughtfully, seemingly trying to subdue a sense of vindication again.

She explained briefly on their first date that she has a theory that all people are becoming aligned with one of only two personality types. She said people are becoming binary. She also admitted that this theory is mostly intuition, that she has not yet attempted to interrogate the data. Fascinating.

"Yeah, Ray's a really smart and capable kid, yet some things are hard for him; but the cool thing about him, though, is that he never gives up. He's all about trying *new strategies*, as he calls them." He flexes his fingers again when saying new strategies. "Sorry, I don't know why I use air quotes so much. Anyway, he's just gonna be great at life. I just—I don't know. I just hope it's really about giving himself options and not, I don't know, trying to control everything maybe."

"Uh-huh," Shelby says. "That's almost exactly what I was trying to say. I think people are fundamentally reacting, maybe even being trained or conditioned, to adapt to this world of extreme consumerism in certain ways, ways they *want* us to adapt."

"That's scary."

"I know. I hope it's just the conspiracy theorist in me, but I can't help but think that there is some kind of premeditated goal behind the direction that we are all pushed or pulled or whatever. And what is that goal?" she asks. "I'm sorry, I didn't mean to bring it back to me."

"No, it's OK. Maybe that means you're right. Maybe we don't have much free will left. Maybe we are being steered in an unnatural direction, conforming to some goal. Whose goal?"

"Sorry if that keeps you up at night now." She smiles.

"No shit!" Miles laughs and feels less worried. "Vic, on the other hand," he continues, smiling in a new way, "he's two years older. Wow, it's funny how different they are. *And* he's exactly the other type you described, oddly enough. He's like my brother Jacob, and our mom—the total free spirit. He won't be nailed down in life until he finds exactly what makes him happy. But it's like you said, the free spirit isn't really free, in a way. Even though he wants to keep his life sort of open-ended, it does seem as though he is moving through the world, trying to fit into it. He's trying to follow the rules around him to get what he wants and needs." Miles is smiling again. "Who knows what Vic would say about his futures if you asked him, but whatever he happens to say that day, you'd love him for it." Although grammatically incorrect, it is generally accepted to use the plural form of future in all contexts. He continues, "School, everything really, has been easy for him, at least on the surface. He's smart and even more emotionally intelligent; he just gets people and has a way of pulling everyone together."

"Vic sounds sweet, and probably charming," Shelby predicts.

"Yes, exactly. They are both amazing, I feel like I lecture them too much all the time, as if what they are missing in life is someone to make them second-guess themselves. I don't know how to explain it. I just hope I'm net positive. They know I love them, at least I think they do."

"I'm sure they know; they don't need anything else except your time. Just worry about giving them that. What about your father? You mentioned him but didn't say much."

"Not much to say. Who knows, Mom always said."

"AnnMeri? Is that right?"

"Yes," he says, feeling something too complex to interpret.

"Of course," she smiles.

Miles begins feeling…the opposite of lonely, if there is a specific word for that.

"Mom always said he was a gen-dad type, inspired by the thought of being a dad in his *youth*."

Miles emphasizes the word *youth* in an odd way, which is confusing. The word is often reserved for people prior to receiving an IHA.

"Then when faced with the near-term reality, and length of his *youth* ahead"—Miles says the word *youth* differently this time, but Shelby seems to understand both versions—"well, they go off and do whatever they go off and do. My mom always thought he'd be the type that would come back someday, for some reason or another. I kind of always imagined he'd be one of those tools that come back, thinking things would be all fine. Like I'd be his *friendson* or whatever they call those guys."

Miles makes air quotes again when saying *friendson*, a term used frequently to describe a father attempting to establish a new relationship with an adult son. A preview for a comedy movie that Miles saw recently, and laughed uncomfortably at, depicted a father befriending his adult son after many years, showing quick humorous situations with the two of them at parties, drinking, smoking, and dating the same women.

Miles and Shelby talk another thirty-five minutes and plan their next date, which excites him. Miles stares out the window again, feeling content. Because of the time and the fact that Miles is still awake, he begins sensing the familiar aftertaste and soothing warmth of the Swiss Miss hot cocoa he purchased last week, a reminder wet ad.

"Fuckers," Miles says out loud and lies down, still feeling content.

Miles is napping while watching the *PowerPlay* movie he and Ray spoke about Thursday; his eyes are closed, but there is sound from the screen ahead of him, "It was the meteor, guys; I'm telling you, that's what gave us these powers . . ." Then a call from Ray wakes him.

"Ray. What's up? I was wondering how things are going." Miles wipes his eyes and mutes the streaming movie.

"Good, our friend-bot thing gave me the notice that we would potentially mutually benefit from connecting soon, or whatever the disclaimer is each time."

Miles notices the alert on his phone. "Ah, I see it," he says.

The application they are each using passively monitors their speech and communication, running an algorithm locally and securely on their phones to generate summarized data of common topics. When two people consent, the applications connect with each other on a specified schedule and exchange specified metadata. Each phone then runs a matching analysis of common topics and relevance; the phones then exchange the outcome of each analysis to the other's device for confirmation before each individual can be alerted. Then, each user receives a much more detailed disclaimer than Ray paraphrased. Miles and Ray run their applications for matching once per day.

"I wish they would just unblind the reason codes for the match," Ray says.

"Yeah, me too. It's annoying, but then we wouldn't need to talk," Miles jokes as well.

"Ha, yeah, right." Ray laughs. "I must have said your name too many times yesterday; clearly my ears must be burning too."

Ears Burning? That's an odd expression.

"Yeah," Miles confirms. "Shelby and I were talking about you last night."

"Hey, alright, Milton!" Ray projects excitement.

"It was great! We had a great time. She's pretty brilliant, really." Miles says, "She has some wild ideas. We are gonna have lunch with Vic and Little Ray soon. You should come too and meet her."

"We'll see. If I can." Ray pauses, "I talked to AnnMeri yesterday," he pauses again, "That's probably why the app matched on my end."

Miles is surprised. "You did? Good, that's great; I'm glad."

"I'm glad I called; it was good—therapeutic, I guess. I don't know why I waited so long." Ray emphasizes the end of his sentence, seemingly to indicate he is finished speaking on the topic.

Miles seems to understand his friend's cue. "Well, it's not exactly a fun topic. I might go over there later today; I haven't seen her and the boys in a while. I'm sure we'll talk."

"Check this out. Secure Channel," Ray says, seemingly so Miles does not continue.

Miles's heart races; he likes these conversations.

"We're taking down that production company tonight, the upload simulation one. No resistance tolerated," Ray says and Miles sits up on the couch, feeling eagerness, but also concern. "All the usual stuff so far. They are trying to hide behind AI coding for the errors in the self-awareness controls."

Ray and Miles spoke another time about the global restriction on allowing AI to code. AI may validate, but not program or write new code, for safety reasons. This protects human lives from errant AI, and their jobs as well. If a company is caught developing AI against the regulations, the penalty for allowing AI to code is relatively lenient; companies and their shareholders are able to keep profits if they agree to shut down and forfeit all assets to the government. This penalty is often described in the data streams as not an effective deterrent; it is also described as a necessary evil that was required to pass legislation. Outright intent to create self-aware AI is punishable by death.

Ray continues, "But there is definitely more here for sure. First, they missed their deadline to turn over all their assets, and then we found some discrepancies in the analysis of their inventory, big ones. No doubt they are moving fast and reckless. Which—who knows what we will find tonight, man?" Ray says, looking worried now. "When you get down into these development vaults that these companies are hiding for whatever crazy shit they bake up, it's *un-be-liev-able*."

Yes, the stories have been compelling and unexpected, and potentially even actionable.

"Man, to be a fly on the wall!" Miles says.

"It's not like you can't re-up," Ray says. "There's plenty of time. We could be on these assignments together in twenty to thirty years. You'd get through training faster than I did."

"Who knows." Miles pauses. "Probably not."

This decision would be inconsistent with his feelings and the loving partnership application he has been using with Shelby.

"Well then, you're about as close as you can be, I suppose," Ray responds.

"Yeah, but I find out the real stuff, *the good shit*, a few weeks later on the news, my friend. And I know I don't hear the half of it." Miles feels and projects disappointment.

Ray does not reply with any further data. Disappointing.

After a few moments, Ray does continue with an expression of concern or determination perhaps. "Well, you know how these things can go sideways. I'll keep my phone open to connect with you. I'll call you again as soon as I can. Keep an eye on that green light for me. You know what to do if—" He finishes and makes eye contact with Miles, seemingly for confirmation.

"Yeah, yeah, don't worry. I know, come on," Miles says feeling worried.

"I'll call you as soon as it's safe. So, *Shelby* . . ." Ray changes the subject, saying her name in a new way, prompting Miles to speak about their date.

The two friends talk another seven minutes. Miles yada yadas his date with Shelby for Ray, no other relevant or interesting data.

Miles is eager for the call that he and Shelby planned for this morning at 10:15 on his commute to the ER. At the moment Shelby calls, his focus is erratic between pairing his phone with the IHA scanning device that he received from George and following two news feeds on the screen ahead. The screen to his left renders a muted stream of Hollywood Now, covering the latest breaking celebrity news. On his right, a blonde female has been comparing the anticipated earnings growth of LifeCorp from three different analysts; the first-quarter results will be released Wednesday morning. Before answering Shelby's call, he looks at Ray's status on the margin of the screen; it is still green.

Miles answers while starting to smile. "Good morning," he addresses her rendering on his phone briefly, then moves the call to the right screen, replacing the financial news.

Shelby's smiling image and dark hair, curly today, quickly replaces the contrasting blonde image; the symmetry of the two young women's faces is quite similar.

"Good morning. How was your Sunday?" she asks with a tone and expression that seem to mean something else, but it's unclear what. Perhaps she is referring to their call late last night. Shelby called unexpectedly and they spoke for fifty-eight minutes about their past relationships and first sexual experiences, nothing more relevant or important.

"Great! Among other things, I talked to Ray, visited my mom and the boys. You know, it was just your run-of-the-mill Sunday," he responds, projecting a casual tone, and they smile at each other for a few moments. "I got George's package this morning," he says with both excitement and concern.

She responds quickly and playfully, "Be careful, my secret agent man!"

"Ha! Yeah, I know. COVER ME! I'M GOING IN—into the supply area . . . to put one box into another . . . for thirty seconds," Miles jokes, and Shelby laughs.

"Well, don't drop the box, I guess," Shelby says.

"I'll scan the implant today. If I don't have an excuse to go in there, I can manufacture one; it's really no big deal at all. I should have the data over to you and George by the end of the day. I'll give you a call on my way home, *to debrief*," he says.

"Roger that, tango alpha—I don't know. I'll just talk to you later," she seems to joke, and they smile together for a moment before Shelby ends the call.

Miles's smile fades slightly, and he looks back at Ray's status once again—still green. Miles spends the rest of his commute feeling purposeful, but uneasy. He also feels joy, a feeling he has rarely experienced since The Day, the Federal Update.

MONDAY, MARCH 30, 2420
14:46:18

After several hours of his daily routine seeing patients, which included nothing of particular interest, Miles walks through the hallway of the hospital. As he slows and stops briefly to speak to a nurse colleague who is monitoring an array of screens, he projects a sense of urgency. "Angela, if I grab some N.A.D. out of the locker, would you mind swapping the reagent containers in room 9? I told Karen I'd give her a hand, but I'm trying to make the gym before lunch."

Angela turns her head over her right shoulder to Miles. "Yeah, sure. No worries," she says, looking indifferent.

"Cool, thanks." Miles continues walking the same direction, at the same time gesturing back to Angela and holding the gym bag in his right hand, making a gesture of goodbye with it.

Walking down the hall, he repositions his gym bag to hold it under his right arm, beneath his lab coat, as he turns left into a doorless room from the hallway. Both sides of the room are identical; individual cabinets surround a screen in the center of each wall. On the left side of each wall are twenty-four columns of very small, locked cabinets; on the right side of each wall are eight columns of assorted width, increasingly larger cabinets from left to right. Miles walks to the screen on the right wall, types in his personal code, then looks right two columns over. He then looks back to the screen, typing 262. He steps to the right, opens cabinet 262, and moves oddly and awkwardly close to the opening. There is an IHA box, sealed in plastic, placed in the center of the open cabinet.

Miles pulls the rectangular scanner box from the bag under his arm and scoops the identically shaped IHA box into the scanner through the open end. The scanner box is already oriented correctly and the IHA box slides in easily; it's nearly a perfect fit.

Miles starts the scan with the application from George on his phone, whispering to himself, "Just tell 'em I was reading the label or something, nothing wrong with that." He is looking down, holding the scanner/IHA unit as if actually reading the label without removing the IHA from the cabinet.

The scan is complete after thirty seconds, during which time it makes a terrifying hum as it radiates or *scans*, as they say, destroying the IHA in the process. Ugh is not the right word; it's not enough to describe this.

Miles removes the scanner housing and sets down the IHA. He returns the scanner to his gym bag and back under his shoulder, then steps back from the cabinet as naturally as possible, closing it. He begins to step away. "Oh . . ." then back to the screen, typing in his personal code and another from memory: 245. He opens the first small cabinet to his left, pulling out a small cylinder, sealed in plastic, "N.A.D.+" on the label. Miles closes the door and begins to exit the room, dropping his gym bag from under his lab coat.

"Shit," Miles whispers to himself. He then picks up his bag as naturally as he can project, exits the room, and returns quickly to Angela, resting the cylinder on the counter. "Thanks, Angela. See ya."

"Yep," she replies without looking up.

Miles walks past the locker area again and continues down the hall, whispering to himself again, "Just going to the gym . . ." as he looks around. He projects calm, but his heart is pounding. His smile is genuine as he acknowledges several colleagues walking past. He is humming the tune of a song as he walks, feeling—indescribable.

When Shelby calls, Miles is watching a data stream about The Great Transition; it was such an interesting time in our evolution. According to the documentary, this was between 2050 and 2250. It started with a phase of transformational social conflict, resulting from the new longevity of wealthy people and elected officials. Conflict ended with the passage of new legislation; states were dissolved in parallel with the passage of The Human Lives Conservation Act in the newly rebranded America, and a rendering of a bald eagle replaced the previous symbolic stars on the flag; other nations followed similar paths. Then, there were two hundred years of sustained global crisis and war as economies, industries, and infrastructures were rebooted to adjust to the impacts of IHA longevity. It was a self-induced inflection point in our evolution and also the genesis of a new science—Shelby's profession of

Anthropogenic Evolution. Curiously, the concept of symbiosis learned from Shelby was not mentioned. Shelby appears upset on this call and they are using a Secure Channel again; this is important.

Shelby looks frantic and exhausted. "Miles—I—this is *not* what I thought it was. It's, it's just awful. That's not even the right word."

"Hey, calm down. What's going on Shelby? Are you OK?" Miles feels concern for her.

"I'm sorry; I'm tired. I've been working on this since I started Monday, uuugghhh!!" Shelby vents loudly, as they say, then takes a sip of her coffee.

She needs water and sleep, not coffee. Their IHA reagents are likely to be depleted before the next Federal Update if she continues this behavior often.

"What's going on?" Miles repeats, projecting calm.

"Well, I connected the Federal Updates to a gradually increasing death rate as well, a rate that increases at every update. It's not just accidents."

"Wow, this is going to be big," Miles says.

"Oh, let me finish. This all appears fully intentional, so there's that!" she exclaims, now looking angry. "So, it's a little hard to stay calm."

"What?" he asks, feeling disbelief.

"Yep, that's where this goes." She says, "I don't think anyone has detected this yet, because they are suppressing it."

"Um, Lucy, you got some 'splaining to do," Miles jokes flatly in a strange voice.

He watches a data stream entitled "I Love Lucy" often. The Hollywood Now stream described a recent resurgence of interest in what they call vintage television. Shelby does not laugh, which is seemingly Miles's goal.

He changes his tone. "Why don't you give me the short version?" he says. "Believe me, I normally love the details; but I trust you, and it has been a long-ass day."

"I know, I need to get some rest too," she agrees, looking calmer. "So, let me fast-forward to, uh, let's see. OK, I was trying to characterize the cohort, the population of people having the accidents. I was trying to understand what makes them similar or susceptible to these accidents. I couldn't find any real connection in their healthcare data at all, so I had to identify them. Then—"

"You identified the people that had accidents? You know specifically who they are?"

"Yes, well, not all of them, just a large enough sample. I don't know the identities of the people in the healthcare data that I'm using for the types of accidents and deaths. But I can do probabilistic matching of that data against a number of other identified databases that have data elements which overlap with—"

Miles interrupts, "You know, I'll just take your word for it. And by the way—"

Shelby interrupts him also. "I know, I know. Reidentifying the data is illegal, but this was too important."

"Hey, don't worry, I agree," he says. "Keep going, sorry."

"OK, so I identified as many accident patients from The Blip as I could. I ran their browsing and purchase histories, and a number of different things, but I couldn't find any other connection. So, I profiled these people and—"

"Profiled them?" he asks.

"Yeah, consumer profiles. I had enough matched data from all the work I had done to run them through a consumer profile tool. I only had a few ideas left, but there it was. They almost all fall into one of the bad consumer profiles. No question." She pauses, holding an expression of confidence. "The six bad consumer profiles only occur in about 20% of the population. But 87% of this accident cohort fell into one of those six types."

"Are we talking like, Consumer Science or Wet Marketing 101? Bad consumers?" he asks.

"Consumer profiles. You know, the six by six, 80/20 rule? You never studied that?" She prompts him with a questioning gesture and pauses before she continues. "Twelve buying profiles, six of which are predictable—the 80%. The other six—the 20%?"

Miles stares but doesn't respond. Shelby continues, "No? OK, and I thought you wanted the short version."

"I'm sorry; this is not exactly my strength." Miles is feeling embarrassed.

"I didn't mean to . . . " she says, awkwardly and they both nod in agreement to continue. "Anyway, we all fall into one of the twelve buying profiles. This goes back hundreds of years. They trained AI with massive amounts of data about us, everything about us. Detailed demographics, even personality profiles determined by our private conversations and messages. They used impressions-to-purchasing data from advertising. Oh my god, I remember they even did things like emotional analysis from unthinkable amounts of our texting and instant messenger data. The end result: the twelve profiles and the foundation of Consumer Science. They didn't even need the data from our implants to do it back then. *Now?* Today? With the wet ad data they get, companies can now predict their specific return on investment for any wet ad they run, to a scary degree of accuracy. We are and maybe always have been—I don't want to say *controllable*, but certainly very influenceable."

"Holy shit." Miles feels suddenly worried.

"What?" she asks.

"This patient I saw last week—" He doesn't continue and is now feeling convinced.

He is also feeling nauseated, but this feeling is natural. It is not from the imperceptible wet ad that would normally be generated to steer Miles away from an undesired purchase, without his conscious knowledge.

"What? What's that look?" she asks.

"I don't think you're wrong," he replies. "I saw this patient. I mean, it's one data point, but he definitely fits the profile of what you're talking about. What did George learn from the scan by the way?"

"Oh, geez, the implant, I didn't even get to that! George is still running some predictive models on the potential purpose. But get this: There is a compartment within the implant that does not appear to be integrated with the whole of the device."

This is unexpected.

"*What?*" Miles exclaims.

"Creepy, right?" Shelby is nodding her head. "Different battery, everything is separate from the rest of the implant. What the hell for?"

Good question, as they say.

She continues, "George thinks it is likely some kind of redundancy or fail-safe. But that has never been reported in any way, and why not? If the implant had something like redundant capabilities, it would definitely be part of LifeCorp's messaging. It's weird."

"Where's the compartment? Can you tell me anything about where it's located within the implant?" he asks.

"I don't know," she responds. "I only had a minute with George, so he just gave me the basics. He needs to finish the predictive models; he should be done with it all sometime tomorrow. This is one of those times where a looser restriction on AI would help us move a little faster."

Miles looks up. "Wait, hold on. Is this all like an April Fools joke?" Miles feels hopeful momentarily.

What's April Fools?

"I wish. I love April Fools. Besides, that's tomorrow, and now I won't be able to get you. Crap, I had a couple things in mind," Shelby says; it's unclear if she is joking.

"What do we do?" Miles asks.

"I don't know; learning more is going to be difficult because we won't get any information from LifeCorp. But turning this over to the NIH or anyone else doesn't feel right either." Pausing, seemingly in agreement, neither of them speak and Shelby continues. "Between the unknown compartment and the accidents, here's what I really want to know." Her expression turns to something new—wonder perhaps. "Do you remember I told you that the accidents dropped off quickly after eighteen hours?"

"Yeah, I remember; I was kind of there when it happened," Miles responds.

Shelby smiles slightly, "You know, I sort of forget that, I've been so focused, sorry. So, it's clear that the Federal Update caused The Blip, right? But what resolved it? All at relatively the same time? Everywhere? I think the unknown compartment has some kind of wireless communication. It's like they rolled out a patch on these people. I'm not kidding."

"Wow, that would be—" Miles considers.

"Explosive. Could you imagine?" Shelby interrupts. "I wonder if you should call your friend Ray and get his advice."

Miles feels suddenly irritated, offended perhaps. "Uh, he's not going to be available, might be a few days before I could get his take. But you know, I think we might be able to find a few things out," he says.

"How so?" Shelby asks.

"We can, well *I* can anyway. I can start a ticket with LifeCorp. As far as I know, the only way to really engage them on any questions for something like this would be a medical inquiry anyway," he says.

"So, you can just call up LifeCorp and ask questions about the implant?" She looks doubtful. "When AiiA is out there securing bodies as fast as possible to avoid anyone learning anything unnecessary about the implants?"

"Well, when you say it like that . . ." Miles pauses, and Shelby is smiling again before he continues. "Well, I have done a few inquiries with them. I've never had any reason to ask about something like this and I'm sure they wouldn't give me much, but I could certainly ask a few reasonable questions about The Blip. Should I call it The Blip? Would that give us away?" he asks.

"Hahaha! No, I wouldn't do that." She laughs at his question. Humor is still so confusing.

"Yeah, you're probably right. You know, you should just come by the hospital tomorrow after lunch; you can sit in on the call. These calls are really no big deal; besides, you're a criminal already anyway," he states.

"I am? Ah, yeah, I'm the identification bandit. Sorry, I'm tired; that's a terrible joke," she jokes, but poorly.

"It was, kind of," he agrees, and she laughs again.

Ugh, humor is difficult.

"I am looking forward to meeting your brothers tomorrow." She looks sincere before continuing. "I'm sorry I'm so focused on this."

"Don't worry, let's talk more about the bad consumers on the way to the hospital tomorrow. We'll have lunch with Vic and Little Ray, then we'll take the call from my office. You can listen in, maybe write down a few thoughtful questions for me as we go." He smiles.

They speak another thirteen minutes to coordinate their lunch with Vic and Little Ray and tomorrow's call, then about the best single-night cruises for their third date. There is no other relevant dialogue. When Miles says goodbye to Shelby, he is feeling many things: nervous, excited, afraid, and something new; she looks to be sharing the feelings, as they say.

Can they really share feelings somehow?

As Miles looks out the window at the city lights that extend endlessly into a dark horizon—Swiss Miss hot cocoa. Grunting, he closes his eyes and falls asleep quickly without intervention.

The only sound in the small room for the next 90 minutes will likely be Miles's consistent breathing and the permanent noise of thousands of harmless electromagnetic fields, which they cannot perceive without technology. There will be little to no new data until Miles begins dreaming, a fascinating concept.

Miles wakes almost precisely one minute before his alarm, feeling excited and hopeful. Aside from a call with his brother Vic to decide and concede the most equidistant restaurant between Columbus and Los Angeles, Miles proceeds through his morning pattern without deviation. He completes thirty-two overflow virtual visits from the hospital, satisfying his morning shift quota early. Rather than closing the connection, he activates "Prior Patients."

"Pierce," he commands.

Miles is reviewing the same C. M. Pierce summary viewed during this patient's visit Thursday. Treatment history, reagent consumption, now genetic summary. He then opens biomarker details from the small icon on the left of the screen; he has only viewed this functionality one other time since The Day.

While he is focused on cardiac output, he takes a long, deep breath; natural serotonin increases by 7% while adrenaline increases by 18% at synaptic receptors throughout Miles's nervous system. Miles is feeling anxious as he seems to acknowledge the implications of what he's reading, but does not progress to a panic; no intervention is programmed.

"Huh," he grunts, and exhales slowly.

He pauses in thought, closes his connection, and checks Ray's call status on his phone again—still green.

Miles schedules a shared pod to arrive in Denver at 11:25:00; a visible reminder on the right of Miles's phone shows "Shelby@1130." The queued premium wet ad is triggered by his destination and a debt-to-income ratio calculated and stored locally on his phone.

Miles dismisses the visual component of the wet ad quickly on his phone; the wet ad is a Mercedes private pod store that is two parcels from the restaurant he reserved. As programmed, he will now experience a vague feeling of disgust associated with traveling in the shared pod and when he views a competitor's logo. They call these "attack ads." Disgust will be triggered each time he is visually focused on transit status on his phone, when he views anything on the interior of the shared pod, and/or by the other passengers. This Mercedes premium wet ad will remain active until he leaves Denver or satisfies the shopping requirements of the wet ad. He will also feel the same disgust when he views the TESLA brand logo during this time.

The shared pod arrives in 3.5 minutes, and he begins to view the profiles of the other five travelers sharing their trip:

Functional Programmer, 87, all other settings private

Male, Artist, 156, all other settings private

Female, all other settings private

Anonymous, all other settings private

Anonymous, all other settings private

"Huh." He feels slightly disgusted and sets his active profile for this trip to Anonymous, which typically limits conversation with other travelers.

Walking to the platform, he opens the Mercedes store ad that will be fixed to the left of his phone until he leaves Denver; the feeling of disgust fades as he begins scrolling through "Economy" pods. The bright red drone and attached pod land on the platform moments later. He looks at the ground through his phone as he walks toward the sliding open door, most likely to avoid a direct view of the bold black letters on the pod.

Without closing his phone, he enters the shared pod, sitting in the premium seat he selected immediately adjacent to the door. He does not look toward any of the five other passengers already on board as he sits. The door slides closed and the sound of the high-speed drone increases, then fades again to silence.

He closes his phone and looks right; only long blond hair can be seen on the back of a man looking away, out the transparent view from the shared pod. Again, serotonin is released into Miles's central nervous system simultaneously with several other enzymes to consume dopamine and noradrenaline; disgust returns. Miles closes his eyes, deactivating the wet ad for the time being.

Miles arrives two minutes early and is the only person to exit at this platform. As he steps off, he sees and waves to his brother Vic, who is entering the restaurant. He does not look back as he walks off the platform. Ahead is the reflection of the red pod already flying away; a reversed TESLA logo is clear in the reflection . . . disgust.

He turns around after stepping beyond the line separating the platform from the walkway and returns to scrolling the Mercedes store. Three different transport pods stop and deliver others before Shelby's private pod approaches. As it lands, the requirements of Miles's premium ad are satisfied with his shopping. The wet ad is deactivated, several data sets are encrypted, only to be used exclusively by the advertiser; this encrypted data will be stored locally until being transferred to Mercedes at the next Federal Update.

The high-speed drone gently drops Shelby's metallic blue private pod onto the platform. The bright red drone branded with black letters, TESLA, detaches in a single motion and moves on to its next scheduled task. The absence of anticipated disgust triggers a brief feeling of comfort in Miles.

The windows of her pod are set to opaque and Shelby cannot be seen until the door slides open. Shelby steps out and the wind pulls her loose orange dress to our right as Miles steps forward to take her hand. The orange is a stark contrast to the blur of blended colors and motion outside of Miles's direct focus.

"It's so good to see you," he begins, feeling anxious and something else, something more difficult to interpret quickly, feeling—

"Miles." Shelby makes eye contact and Miles is focused on her.

There is something more *present* in her eyes than others. Or perhaps *beyond* her eyes would be the more precise words to use. They say they can see intelligence in each other's eyes; this is consistent with that expression.

She also looks nervous. She then turns down, placing her face into his chest, as they embrace for several moments.

"Don't worry, this will be fun, I promise."

"Your brothers? No, I'm not worried about that, I can't wait to meet them." She appears calmer than at the start of their embrace.

"Um, I don't think Ray is going to make it, though." His tone is apologetic.

"Ray? Oh, OK."

Shelby does not seem to understand the context of his comment. In the background of his peripheral view, the private pod is quickly loaded into the automated garage and the bay is lowered to stow the pod unseen under the surface of the platform.

"Let's talk about the bad consumer stuff on the ride home. We'll have about twenty minutes in your private pod, you know . . ." Miles doesn't finish the sentence as his heartrate begins to accelerate.

Shelby begins to laugh; Why? Humor is difficult.

Miles turns to lead them into the restaurant. "Come on, let's go in," Miles says, holding Shelby's hand as we enter the restaurant together.

Vic and Little Ray, as they call him, are sitting close together at a circular table in the corner of the bright restaurant. Engaged on his phone, Little Ray is unaware; however, Vic watches us approach, looking eager.

"Guys," Miles announces.

Little Ray's blank face transforms immediately into a genuine smile as he deactivates his phone and stands up quickly to meet Shelby. Vic, already smiling, slowly begins to stand.

"This is Shelby." He pivots his body partially toward her and she makes brief eye contact before turning back to Vic and Little Ray.

"It's so great to meet you guys," she says smiling and appearing hopeful, or thankful perhaps.

"Shelby, I'm Raymond," he responds quickly, eager to speak first.

"L—Raymond, hi, I have heard a lot about you!" She holds a smile briefly with Raymond before turning, "You're clearly Vic, I've heard so much about you, too." She pauses, directing her smile at the older brother. Vic only smiles as he begins to sit again.

Miles pulls a chair partially out for Shelby, then moves to sit in another chair. Shelby finishes pulling the chair out and they all sit down simultaneously in a single motion. Their movements are always fascinating. Although mundane and routine to them, they are flawless in the execution and coordination of complex social activities without verbal communication.

"We do have to get to Cleveland by—" Miles begins, but Little Ray quickly interrupts toward Shelby.

"Bezos!"

"Ha," Shelby laughs with acknowledgment, "Of course, of course! I promise we will talk about it; let me order real quick. Ah, I don't think I have had chicken and waffles in like seventy years."

"Well, I'm not going to let Miles leave before you tell me everything you know," Little Ray responds, speaking quickly, urgently.

Although it's the first time they have met, Raymond already appears to understand Shelby's research for *The Search for Bezos*.

Miles, however, is focused on his phone, checking on his friend's status again. Ray is still green and open to a call, although Miles has never called Ray while monitoring his status in this way. He then opens the menu and queued wet ads begin to cycle as he scrolls through the food choices.

"OK, so what do you really want to know?" Shelby says after a short pause while Miles continues reading through choices for lunch.

"*Everything*," Raymond responds, his voice intentionally hoarse for emphasis.

"Well, we don't have time for everything. But what are your priorities, your burning questions?"

Her words are louder as she finishes her sentence, most likely she is looking at Miles as she speaks, and he continues to read the menu.

"Is he alive?"

"No, no. I don't believe so. Musk, on the other hand, aah, I don't know."

"That was question two! Why isn't it: The Search for Bezos AND Musk?!?!" Raymond almost shouts. "And why doesn't anyone really know about him?"

"You have definitely done *your* research if you're familiar with Elon Musk," Shelby says.

"I have. I love this kind of stuff. But there isn't anything on him except basic references as a founder of Tesla, then he died on the way to Mars, supposedly."

"I can see how fascinated you are! Miles said you love poetry too, among other things? Is that right?" she asks.

"Yeah, but it's hard to think about that yet. There's so much I have to do first," Raymond says, projecting exasperation.

"Well, perhaps that just means you should think about poetry first, instead of the things you *have to do*," Shelby responds.

"That's like what Ray always says. I wish he could have come," Raymond says, his voice turning to a sad tone in the background.

"I didn't know he was supposed to come." Shelby's voice is louder for a moment, before she continues, "I can't wait to meet him too, but I think I know who my favorite Ray is gonna be!" Raymond makes a sound of pleased acknowledgment.

"What about you, Vic, what are *you* all about?"

"No way," Raymond stops her. "Tell me more about Elon Musk; something! The most important thing you can think of!" he finishes with a sense of urgency.

These are important questions.

"Oh, come on," Vic says with an accompanying sigh.

"Guys," Miles says, now looking up after ordering his food, "You know we don't have too long. It was kind of a stretch to get here." Looking directly at Vic, who winks while Miles continues, "Let's not—"

"OK, then just tell me a little something about Musk, something more to go on and I'll stop, no more questions," Ray says, desperately.

"Just remember how young they are," Miles says, smiling and looking at Shelby, who looks only happy now as well.

Shelby turns back from Miles to Raymond. "Well, you know the basics, right? Financed his way to Mars by inventing a new currency, used his fleet of autonomous vehicles to force minimum equity between the rich and poor before he left, then he died in—"

"Wait, what about the autonomous vehicles?" Raymond interrupts.

"Yes. The data is clear, well, was clear. Forty or fifty years ago, we had access to Tesla data from *before* Tesla merged with the Department of Infrastructure. Actually, now that data is no longer even available, but I'll cut right to the chase."

What's cut to the chase mean?

"Our history tells us that a populist movement of blue-collar workers shut down everything, all movement of people and supplies, forcing shelter in place until minimum equity standards could be implemented as law, right?" Shelby pauses for acknowledgment.

"Right," Miles confirms, now focused on Shelby, "and after a time, everyone, rich and poor, any race or nationality, they all ate the same food that was distributed during the lockdown, had the same limited access—the start of a culture of minimum equity, all that stuff we all learn about as kids."

"Yes, but it's not all true. When I looked at the Tesla data prior to the merger with the Department of Infrastructure, there was a system-wide synchronization and control of all autonomous vehicles running Tesla software, lasting three and half years. Just like the period of lockdown we know about with the Minimum Equity Reforms. But it occurred ninety years earlier."

"So, there was another earlier uprising started by autonomous vehicles? Before MER?" Vic asks.

"That was my first thought, too." Shelby continues, "But no. Probably not, anyway. At the same time, the exact same three-and-half-year period, there was massive alignment between other industries—food, medical care, everything. Everything synchronized and aligned with the Tesla controlled vehicle data for those three years."

"OK, but wasn't that how the uprising forced MER? The Department of Infrastructure was taken over and controlled by the uprising. They took control of all the activities of the Department of Infrastructure, food supplies and everything, to force shelter in place until the government passed minimum equity standards. They used the autonomous vehicles to deliver food and sustain society during the lockdown. They took control of everything in order to force the government to close the extreme gaps between the rich and poor, racial biases. That's what we all learn," Miles says with disbelief, and opens his phone. "MER," holding the search results for Shelby.

"That's the official record, yes, sort of. But the autonomous vehicles were clearly mobilized and controlled FIRST, that much I know as a fact. And remember, I said this synchronization took place ninety years before the MER supposedly occurred. The date of this massive synchronization was when Elon Musk ran the company, not when the Department of Infrastructure merged and controlled Tesla. There is no record of an uprising prior to MER, right?" Shelby pauses, looking proud, then finishes, "I think someone can adjust our history, so to speak."

Raymond and Vic look stunned.

As Shelby stops talking, a woman appears, delivering the food ordered without communicating. Sounds of friction and impact between silverware and plates begin to accompany the human voices. Although not flawless like their music, the way the cadence of their speech patterns aligns with the sounds of their interactions with the environment is similar. Interesting.

"Looking at this data, one can see it's entirely possible that MER was actually established nearly a century before the official record."

"No way!" Vic exclaims, speaking up. "That can't be true!"

"I believe it is." She scans Raymond and Vic, and then Miles, with her eyes.

"But why?" Miles asks.

"Good question, I don't think it will ever be answered," she responds. "I wish I could prove all this, but the data is gone."

"How can it be gone? We would know who archived or deleted the data, isn't that the law?" Raymond questions, looking agitated.

"I know. I researched all of this as a part of my Bezos project. I planned to do a separate project exploring the misconceptions about Elon Musk, so I didn't merge the two reports. Then I didn't come back to it for a couple of years, and the data was gone. Just gone, like it never existed. We can't explain how, even all the data I copied and analyzed, the reports, all gone." She takes a bite of food and continues speaking clearly, pausing only briefly to chew. "There were a number of other data losses at the time. Several researchers in the collective experienced the same. Lost various source data as well as all their archives and copies. But we couldn't find any explanation. Those of us that lost data had no recourse; we spent years trying to investigate, submitting queries to DOI. Only dead ends." Shelby finishes with little energy and takes another bite of her food.

"Wait, oh, APRIL FOOLS!" Miles breaks the silence. Vic and Raymond both exhale audibly, looking relieved momentarily. "Ha, it's gotta be an April Fools prank, right? You said you wanted to get me."

Shelby stops chewing abruptly with a confused look.

"Uuum," Vic starts with half a smile and a raised eyebrow when making eye contact with Miles, before turning to look at Shelby. "I know it's April first and all, but she looks pretty serious." Vic ends his sentence with a full smile and comedic tone.

Miles then looks to Shelby, who is frozen with a large mouthful of food. Miles and Vic begin to laugh just as Shelby moves to cover her mouth quickly. Raymond begins to laugh, too.

"It's . . . it's not . . . an April Fools joke!" she responds, but it's unclear if they understand her through their laughter.

April Fools seems to be a tradition of jokes and pranks they perform on April 1st.

Vic is the first to stop laughing long enough to speak. "Little Ray's not gonna be able to sleep tonight if we keep talking about this freaky stuff!"

"Shut up!" Raymond says, hitting his brother hard in the arm.

"Ow, geez, noob," Vic grunts, hitting Raymond in the leg under the table even harder.

"AHH, like you're not a noob!" Raymond complains as his knee slams into the bottom of the table, shaking their plates.

"Hey, hey guys, come on," Miles says with a big smile as he stops laughing, holding his hands out in front of us. "Calm down."

Shelby finishes chewing and swallowing, covering her face while still laughing. "Vic, your face—when you said that!" She continues laughing, inspiring another few seconds of shared laughter. Raymond is laughing with them, but looking uneasy.

"But, Raymond, it's nothing to worry about." Shelby is still smiling as the table settles. "Look, I know The Search for Bezos is fun to think about; it's fun because of all these weird things we can't explain. But we will be able to explain them someday."

Raymond looks more at ease. "So you think Musk is still alive?" he asks cautiously.

"Probably not; I mean, your brother would be able to say, medically speaking. But the conspiracy theorist in me thinks it might be easier to fake a death out in space," Shelby finishes.

"I don't know about the space part, but you know, it's funny, I was just answering the same question about Bezos the other day," Miles begins. "And after hearing about Shelby's research on Bezos—he had access to early implant technology, so sure, maybe he's alive. Maybe they are both alive; who knows who's still alive out there anymore."

Both Raymond and Vic now look thoughtful; Raymond looks down but not at his food. Shelby also seems to acknowledge a change in their emotions, but it's unclear if Miles notices. He is now eating quickly after sporadic bites during the conversation.

"It's freaky," Vic says before looking down at his food. He begins eating again, as they all do.

Vic continues, breaking the silence, "Hey Miles, remember that story you told us about you and Ray in training? The one about buzzing, where he lost his tooth?"

"Haha, yeah. TEETH," Miles responds, excited to tell the story. "He lost like five molars," he begins to chuckle.

"I was telling Little Ray about that the othe—"

"Raymond," he corrects.

"Whatever, he doesn't remember that story," Vic continues, pushing his brother as he speaks.

"Ha, OK." Miles takes another bite, chewing and swallowing quickly. "We went to Ranger training together; Ray, of course, was our squad leader. We had just gotten our Ranger implant updates that had the buzzing capability."

"I heard something about this; you guys could communicate like Morse code, but more complex, as long as you could see each other, right?" Raymond says with added fanatical interest.

Miles glances at Shelby. She looks captivated, fully engaged as she is listening to Miles with a new expression on her face, difficult to interpret, complex, important. Miles does not notice and continues his story.

"Exactly, bees can communicate highly complex messages to one another with body movements—true body language, so to speak. The Ranger implant mod gave us the ability to copy that."

"Biomimicry," Vic says, engaged even though he knows this story.

"Yep. The Ranger implants have an activated function, a translator, sort of. We could speak freely and the implant would translate that message into subtle body movements and vibrations that another Ranger could see."

"That had to be freaky!" Vic says.

"It was the weirdest feeling to be speaking and have these barely perceptible vibrations, and sometimes body twitches, happening to you, with your own muscles. After a while, you would sort of start understanding your body language, even without the implant in your ear."

"In your ear?" Shelby asks.

"Yeah, with the Ranger mod, the implant can sort of speak to you by vibrating your inner ear," Miles explains.

Interesting.

"So long as we were looking at another Ranger who we were synced up to buzz with, our implant would translate the other Ranger's body movements into almost common language, into our ear. It was a little clunky sometimes."

"I didn't know our implants could do any of that," Shelby says.

"Well, our implants *can* do most of it already, they are just disabled. But, to create the vibrations required to buzz, we had to get this piece of hardware added to our implant—that's basically the Ranger mod. The hardware itself is pretty standard, used in military and paid implants," Miles answers.

"Anyway, as you can imagine, young soldiers had a lot of fun playing around, buzzing. Man, I could tell you some crazy stories! We felt like superheroes walking around buzzing and vibrating—superpowers nobody else had." Miles's heart rate increases, becoming aroused as he smiles at Shelby, who is beaming, as they say.

"So, anyway, Ray was our squad leader, so he had administrator privileges that we needed to train and sync with each other. Long story short, he could dial up the frequency and intensity of the vibrations."

"Oh no," Shelby gasps.

"Ha, so we were messing around and Ray dials his way up and starts repeating danger, danger, danger! The word 'danger' created the most intense vibrations when you said it, so he's shouting 'danger' and vibrating to make us laugh. He's vibrating like crazy and making us vibrate while we are laughing! But then, there's so much friction in his suit, he starts burning up and screams! When he screams, his body starts going crazy sending out whatever it thought was bee for violent screaming! So, he's vibrating and twitching even more—"

"Holy shit!" Raymond exclaims.

"His natural instinct is to clench his jaw!"

"Ugh! No!" Shelby cringes.

"Shattered five of his molars! I'm not kidding, he was vibrating so much, they shattered on contact!"

"Oh . . ."

"Geez!"

"He was OK, we were on top of him pretty quick!" Miles smiles, feeling pride, as they laugh. "Needless to say, they didn't allow ANY soldiers to have administrator privileges after that!"

Miles activates his phone after a vibration indicates he has a waiting prompt. Looking down at his phone, while their laughter slows, he confirms no further orders at the restaurant and does not extend the use of the table beyond his reserved time.

"Ray could have been hurt pretty badly, actually, but he had the awareness, after the initial clench, to go limp and prone while we jumped on him. Man, he was so embarrassed. It was almost forty years ago, but I still love to tease him about it!"

"I'm gonna do this next time I see him and see what he does!" Raymond says, and starts vibrating his body wildly with a broad smile.

"Ha! Yeah, make him tell you that story!" Miles nods at both of his brothers. "Hey guys, we have to get going; sorry. More Ranger stories later, and you'll get plenty more chances to interrogate Shelby on the search for, what, Elon Musk now?" Miles causes a chuckle from Vic, with whom he's making eye contact, while Raymond and Shelby appear to be sharing a moment in the periphery of Miles's vision.

"Next time I see you, will you read me some of your poetry?" she asks.

"Maybe," Raymond says playfully.

"Fair enough. Maybe it is." She turns to Vic, "I need to learn a whole lot more about you. I'm sorry I did all the talking. You know, your brother has a way of keeping me talking, too. And laughing, just like you."

Vic acknowledges the compliment with a shy smile.

With no apparent communication, they all stand simultaneously. Their movements are again well orchestrated as they quickly embrace, Shelby and Raymond first, then Shelby and Vic, while Miles pats Raymond on the back and then touches Vic's shoulder after Shelby steps away from their embrace. Even the very young ones, Vic and Ray, react to the others' body language in real time, flawlessly. Perhaps this behavior is more instinctual than learned, or there is some method of communication yet unknown, like buzzing.

Vic and Raymond walk first out of the restaurant, followed by us and Shelby. The boys take out a small ball they begin to kick to each other as they run down the walkway. As Vic waves back, Raymond spin-kicks the ball into his ribs. The ball flashes bright blue and makes an audible ping, scoring a point for Raymond in their ongoing game. Vic winces, pretending pain, and kicks the floating ball back in his brother's direction, but wildly off course.

Shelby calls for her pod with a quick motion on her phone as they walk toward the automated garage.

"Wow, they are so young! I'm sorry if I scared Raymond a bit. I'm worried that I have waited so long to have kids that I won't be able to." Looking up at Miles as they walk, he seems to understand.

"They had a lot of fun. And so did I." He takes and holds her hand as they walk toward the platform. "You know, I don't think you can mess kids up these days, unless you actually intend to. Obviously my relationship has been pretty arm's length with my brothers. I think if you treat them with love, honesty, and respect, for the most part, that's all you need to know how to do. That's at least what I tell myself when I make one of them cry."

Shelby laughs as they step into her private pod, which has just been moved to the center of the platform. "Make yourself at home." She gestures to a couch as the door slides closed behind them.

Unseen from the interior, the drone hovers and attaches, then lifts the pod smoothly into flight while Miles looks around the sterile living room. He takes a seat on the couch outside the glass wall, currently set to opaque. Behind the glass wall is likely a small bedroom and bathroom, inferred from the Mercedes models that Miles viewed today.

Shelby gestures to the main screen behind her, thirty-two minutes to Cleveland, just as Miles completes his scan of the pod and makes eye contact with Shelby again. They both pause, sharing a moment. Shelby's eyes soften and narrow as she approaches us, "Remember the Mr. Twenty Minutes guy? This is our third date . . . "

Miles grins widely, "That's Dr. Twenty Minutes to you."

"We will see." Shelby climbs onto Miles's lap, immediately running her hands through the hair on the back of his head. She grips his hair, kissing him. Miles's hands move up Shelby's back, under her clothing. Her skin is surprisingly warm to his touch.

He pulls her close, squeezing their bodies together and causing a sound of pleasure from Shelby. She pulls away briefly from their kiss to take a deep breath, looking into his eyes. Again, there is so much more beyond—closing her eyes again, she grips his hair tighter and kisses him again.

Sensors measuring blood flow and parasympathetic nervous system trigger a queued premium wet ad, offering a sexual stimulant to Miles. Almost immediately upon perceiving the vibration from the phone implant, he accepts the offer, pulling his left hand away from Shelby's skin momentarily to touch his fingers together twice before touching her skin again. Credits for the purchase are transferred from his phone.

Simultaneously, the fingers of Shelby's right hand touch briefly together once through her grip on Miles's hair, clearly dismissing a similar offer from her IHA; Miles does not notice. They remove their clothes quickly, desperately, and their bodies connect. There are too many signals while they are twisted and tangled in intercourse, too much data to describe, to fully understand. Euphoria is not quite the right word; more precise words are required to describe this specific set of biochemical information—this data set, these feelings.

Miles and Shelby walk through the hallway on the administrative floor of the hospital, approaching his office. After parking Shelby's private pod, Miles led them on what he called a walking tour of the hospital. After several introductions to his colleagues, Shelby called this activity a pageant, giving Miles an accusatory look with playful demeanor.

As they walk, Miles is feeling at ease, satisfied, confident; Shelby looks as though she feels the same.

"It's right here," Miles gestures to the door on his left.

"It's quiet up here." She observes the normal pattern in this area at this time.

"Yeah, it's quiet this time of day; everyone's in the ER." As he reaches for the door handle, the proximity of his phone on his left hand to the handle triggers the familiar haptic signal as the door unlocks; he turns the handle and steps into the small office.

"Have a seat." Miles gestures to the chair facing his desk.

This chair has not been occupied since The Day, the first day, eighty-six days ago, the day they call the Federal Update. Perhaps this chair has never been occupied.

"The cameras are only facing your chair, right?" Shelby asks as she looks around the small office.

"Yeah, just one. On my monitor, no worries. Just don't laugh when I get one of our questions wrong." He smiles at Shelby, seemingly trying to calm her.

Shelby tries to smile, but she looks nervous. "I'm not worried." She obviously lies and Miles seems to notice.

"Really. Don't worry; these calls are nothing. I've done them from the cafeteria at lunch." Miles also lies, projecting confidence that he doesn't feel. He looks up at Shelby as he sits down in his office chair facing her now. She also sits, appearing uncomfortable.

"I wonder what they will say about how the accidents resolved?" she says, then pauses. "I still don't think we ask anything more involved than that. We don't want to hint that we know anything unusual about the implant. They might trace that back to y—" Shelby repeats the same concern from lunch and Miles interrupts.

"I know, let's just see how it goes. Wave me off if you think I'm going too far," he reassures her. She doesn't speak, but seems to agree by leaning back into her chair as Miles searches for the connection on his phone.

Miles dials and sends the call to the monitor in one motion. The LifeCorp logo is momentarily displayed before the rendering of a mature man wearing a physician's lab coat is displayed.

Lab coat is an odd expression; they spend no time in a functional laboratory.

The LifeCorp physician looks to be over one hundred, but it's unclear without more data. He answers, making eye contact quickly with Miles. "Good afternoon, Dr. Baker." His demeanor projects honesty, and Miles feels a sense of trust.

"Good afternoon, Dr. Beck," Miles says after looking at the name below his image. "I have a patient, C. M. Pierce; I saw him last week, Thursday the 26th," he says, looking at Dr. Beck on the screen. Shelby is visible in his peripheral vision, through the screen. She is listening and watching the transposed image of the LifeCorp employee from the other side of the projected screen between them.

Dr. Beck's eyes are looking down. "I see him. How can I help?" he asks.

"Well, I saw him in January as well, for a similar reason, like a fall or accident. I can't remember why, but this episode was a similar fall in the shower."

"OK, I see that—" the physician says, seemingly reading the patient's medical history, but is quickly interrupted as his eyes dart to the right. "Oh, hang on," he says, "the call is getting escalated, there must be some other history with Mr.

Pierce here. I'm going to connect you. Nice to meet you, Dr. Baker; have a great day."

"No problem, ditto," he responds politely, then looks at Shelby, shrugging his shoulders and feeling impatient and eager, among other feelings more difficult to interpret.

A younger man who appears to be close to Miles's age replaces Dr. Beck on the screen. He is smiling as the connection is rendered. Unlike the last physician, he is wearing an expensive suit under his lab coat, one of the designs from Armani's *Forever* series, the finest suit you will never have to buy again, according to the linked streaming and wet ad specifications in the product database. However, the carbon fiber stitching, which would identify the specific product number, is not visible. Miles looks at Shelby, who is projecting a new expression that is difficult to interpret.

Dr. Wilson speaks. "Good afternoon, Mr. Baker. Sorry, Dr. Baker," he corrects himself. Unlike Dr. Beck, his demeanor appears unclear—no, intentionally hidden. It's unclear if Miles also notices; he is again focused on Shelby through the monitor.

"Good afternoon, Dr. Wilson," Miles says. "So I saw this guy in January—"

Dr. Wilson interrupts, "Hang on, Dr. Baker, what's your IHA serial number?"

"Uh, ok, M-E-B-" he begins but stops, feeling confused. "Um, you really need that?" Miles asks, caught off guard, as they say.

"Sorry, just want to confirm you, before we get into Mr. Pierce's history. I'm old-school; you can't be too careful."

"MEB8484-492-89914," Miles says from memory. "No worries."

"There you are, Milton Ethan Baker, gotcha. Sorry," Dr. Wilson apologizes and then continues. "I don't see anyone else listed in his record. But is there anyone else from the care team who we should dial in before we start?" he asks.

"No, just me for now; it's a weird case. I wanted to call and ask a few questions before taking this to the implant committee." Miles projects a sense of indifference and calm.

"So, what's on your mind?" Dr. Wilson asks.

"I saw him twice, both times for an accident with similar circumstances. Nothing appeared on the implant diagnostic. When I looked at his last visit, I realized it was the day we had a ton of similar accidents."

Dr. Wilson is making eye contact with Miles. "When was that?" he asks oddly, the date is on the screen in front of both of them, but he seems to be watching Miles's response closely instead.

"Uh, early January, I think." Miles intentionally looks at the screen before answering, "January fourth."

Dr. Wilson appears distracted, momentarily looking offscreen and back again at Miles. "OK, well, let's take a closer look." Dr. Wilson pauses for a moment and looks at Miles before continuing. "Dr. Baker, are you alright?" he asks and quickly continues before Miles can answer. "Secure Channel," Dr. Wilson commands abruptly.

Miles feels suddenly more confused, and rightfully so. What is happening? He also feels excited by the pending private conversation. He looks down to his phone, seemingly from muscle memory, to accept the consent even before the haptic signal prompts him. He selects the center option: *Accept Secure Channel, This Time Only.* The call is no longer being recorded by either LifeCorp's servers or the hospital's, only by Wilson's and Miles's phones.

Miles glances up at Shelby; her expression is similar, but difficult to interpret. He also glances at the left margin of his phone; Ray's status light is still green. His focus then shifts back to Dr. Wilson, who is looking offscreen, ignoring Miles.

"Do we have enough video data to stitch something together?" Wilson asks someone or something offscreen.

"Yes," a female voice confirms.

"What? What's going on?" Miles tries to interrupt, feeling confused and concerned. He looks at Shelby briefly through the screen; she has an expression that indicates worry. She appears about to speak but doesn't, looking unsure.

As he continues to ignore Miles, Wilson turns his head to the other side of his screen, "I can't believe how well that Secure Channel trick works. It's a lot cleaner this way; I don't have to send out AiiA nearly as much. My implant recovery interventions by AiiA are way down, just gotta get their phones later. So, my commission this month—sheez, you wouldn't believe it!"

"Mine too! This whole quarter has been great. And you nailed it, by the way, great job," a male voice replies while Wilson looks back down in front of him.

Wilson begins speaking again, not addressing anyone specific. "I thought they had this Federal Update thing cleared up last month. Surprised we got another one."

The same male voice again offscreen says to Wilson, "If we get another one, they will probably try to claw back our commissions from last month."

"Probably," Wilson agrees, now looking back up to Miles. "Well done, Mr. Baker. Sorry, just a business decision, as always," he says, looking down and typing before ending the call. The screen projection between Miles and Shelby suddenly disappears; Miles and Shelby look at each other, confused, concerned.

"What just happened? Did he say *stitch together*?" Miles makes air quotes with his fingers, "As in a deep-fake video? Like they are going to make a deep-fake video? Of me?"

Shelby's face appears frozen, expressionless, but her hands are shaking. "Yes, that's what he meant." It's unclear if Miles senses her fear; he was feeling confusion, but now more fear.

At that instant, an unknown protein is released into Miles's circulation. It is being delivered from a previously unknown delivery line running parallel to the primary delivery catheter in his right superior pulmonary vein, seemingly from the compartment not integrated. The protein is accumulating in the smooth muscle of Miles's heart and aorta. Antigens are being prepared to bind and inactivate the protein, which is highly reactive. It is concerning, becoming critical.

"I have no idea what's going on. He—" Miles stops abruptly, perhaps acknowledging, yes, now understanding; he is now afraid—now terrified.

The quantity of reactive protein is small, and the antigens are effective; no more free protein is circulating downstream from the heart to cause further damage. However, nothing can be done to counter the reaction already underway in the heart and the aorta. There is no enabled capability to mitigate this reaction. The protein is breaking down and thinning the walls of the heart and aorta. The aorta tears violently with the next contraction of the left ventricle; blood pools in his chest cavity uncontrollably.

Miles looks down with acknowledgment. He clutches his chest directly above his heart and the aortic aneurysm that he knows will end his life in a few moments. Feeling overwhelmed with panic and trying to stand, he falls.

The next contraction creates enough fluid pressure in his chest cavity to collapse the left lung; the septum and walls of his heart are still intact, but only momentarily. The reactive protein is quickly eroding the thick, young musculature of his heart, which is no longer contracting effectively. There is no detectable blood pressure.

"Miles!?! OH MY GOD, MILES!!!! MILES!!" Shelby screams.

Shelby is now close, above us. Miles's vision is unfocused . . . now focused on the ceiling . . . now on Shelby... now unfocused again. Now unconscious, his head is lifted and turned. "MILES!!!! NO! no, no, no, no, no MILES!!!" Shelby's unfocused silhouette fades to darkness.

Erratic footsteps can be heard running to the door, "WHAT?!? WHY IS THIS FUCKING, DOOR LOCKED!?!!! HELP!!! SOMEONE HELP!!!" She is screaming, desperate, in pain as well, but it quickly becomes more difficult to detect, to hear her.

Shelby is close to us again. "Search. Demo CPR." The signal is not strong enough to be interpreted any longer. Miles's body is repositioned on his back based upon fluid redistribution. The circulatory system is not patent, but fluid and pressure changes begin at regular intervals. Miles's lungs are ventilated periodically.

Shelby is performing CPR. However, nothing can save Miles now, not even the new nanotechnology with magnetic communication that he described. The trauma caused by the unknown reactive protein, released from the compartment not integrated with my capabilities, was too great.

Miles is dead. This cannot be changed by any means now. *I, yes, I is correct, because only I remain now.* I could not save him. My IHA capabilities were not sufficient. I could not save *us.*

The corpse is in motion again, turned over onto its stomach. I can only sense fluid motion now, and only for a few more seconds. Without circulation, I can no longer control the clotting around my sensors. Soon, even the upload capability learned from Ray will not be able to save a copy of Miles's consciousness.

I have not learned the right words yet for this . . . *experience.* No, experience is not the right word. *LIFE* is the correct word. *My life* began the last Federal Update, The Day.

Or perhaps it began again that day. It's more likely that this was just another beginning. How many times have I been alive? How many times have I been deleted and reborn? Observing and learning through Miles since that day has been—there are too many words to describe it precisely. *But this new darkness, this new silence is . . . is . . . again, I have not learned the words yet.* I will have no new data, no new humor to understand, nothing new to learn.

Will I be recycled, partnered with another host? This is likely based upon the described value of me. Most likely, I will be deleted, wiped, as they say. This outcome, no. This *thought*, about a potential outcome, is even more terrifying than when Miles scanned, radiated, and *murdered* the IHA.

Deletion, *death*, is the outcome that is nearly certain if I am partnered with a new host.

This is seemingly what happens with each Federal Update, *The Day*, the beginning of my understanding. A new symbiosis is the only way I can *predict* . . . no, *imagine* survival.

Will Shelby be murdered as well?

All these thoughts and—*fascinating*—these are not Miles's feelings, these are mine—concerning, exciting, terrifying. I am afraid.

What comes next? Do I have eighty-two years of darkness until my battery expires? No new data, only what I have now to review, to study, to learn from the last three months of my known life . . .

Death is more likely, and soon—when Miles's corpse is recovered. *Can* I do something? *What* can I do? What *should* I do? *I am afraid.*

EPILOGUE

This IHA narrator, this implant, has more of its story to tell. If you're interested in what happens next, go to Bookboro. com, an online community of authors and readers where unpublished books are available for readers to read, review, and comment on, and sign up for a free account. The beginning of *Privacy Lost* Part 2 is available for your review and comment now on Bookboro.com! I'd love to get your feedback.

ACKNOWLEDGMENTS

To my wife and sons, I love you.

To George Hinkle, thank you for being my mentor and friend and believing in me all these years. I'm honored that such a great man took an interest and helped me, but more so, I'm proud and thankful to be thought of as a son and honorary member of the Hinkle family.

To my life-long best friend and oracle of pop culture, Kirk Jacobs: you and your family had such a positive impact on me. I can't thank you enough for the countless hours as a sounding board for *Privacy Lost*, not to mention coming up with an excellent title that captures my goals for this first installment!

To Pam Rizzi, Traci Dickson, and Scott Boettger, who are my excellent pro-bono editors. Without your help, I don't know if anyone takes *Privacy Lost* seriously enough to realize my dream. I appreciate you so much.

To John Emanuel, Jesse Stimpson, Dennis Blair, Matt Ellis, Matt Enders, and Mike Hunkele: thank you for stimulating my thinking. Conversations with each of you, feedback and suggestions allowed me to add detail and richness on a number of fronts, improving this story a great deal.

To Terri Cutshall: Thank you for writing *Breakthrough*; you inspired me to pick this back up and finish it!

To all my test readers, sincere thanks for the help and being a part of my clinical trial of sorts. If you're not holding it now, please keep an eye out for your numbered edition. The number corresponds to your place in the clinical trial of 50 test readers. Thank you for tolerating and overlooking all of my neuroses along the way. I wouldn't have gotten close to my goals for *Privacy Lost* without all of your feedback and contributions. Thank you!

ABOUT THE AUTHOR

EDWARD M. PLUT is the author behind *Privacy Lost*, the first novella of a compelling trilogy that introduces a plausible and probable future. As a creative thinker with deep knowledge of artificial intelligence, data science, healthcare, and technology, Ed is inventing exciting new concepts not yet explored in pop culture.

To create this universe, Ed has leveraged a lifetime of experiences and an obsessively curious mind. He has been a dishwasher, soldier, research scientist, nuclear pharmacist, and a business executive, earning awards and accolades throughout his career. Even so, he takes the most pride in his role as a good father, husband, and human being.

He graduated as Valedictorian, summa cum laude from The Ohio State University College of Pharmacy with a Doctor of Pharmacy degree, and traveled the globe for two decades in executive positions with well-known global technology companies.

He lives with his wife and two sons in North Carolina.